The Faery Garden

The Faery Garden

Beatrice Phillpotts

PALAZZO

This edition published in Great Britain in 2010 by

PALAZZO EDITIONS LTD
2 Wood Street
Bath, BA1 2JQ
United Kingdom

www.palazzoeditions.com

Design and layout copyright © 2010 Palazzo Editions Ltd.
Text copyright © 2010 Palazzo Editions Ltd.

Art Director: Bernard Higton
Illustrator: Kim Glass

A CIP catalogue record for this book is available from the
British Library.

ISBN 978-0-95644-483-7

Printed and bound in Singapore by Imago.

Contents

Part One

Then And Now

Deep in the heart of nature there exists an enchanted otherworld.
Its powerful magic has been a part of our lives since time immemorial,
but its form and shape are as elusive as a dream. Nothing is what
it seems in faeryland. It can be here, there, everywhere.
Through the centuries, however, it has most frequently manifested
itself as a beautiful but perilous garden within a garden. The hidden
entrances, as folk legend reveals, are always unexpected.
The way in can be over the hills and far away, or just beyond
the next bend. Its enchanted portals may be a towering tree,
a single flower, or even the space between.

Garden of Delights

> 'Come away, O, human child!
> To the woods and waters wild,
> With a fairy hand in hand,
> For the world's more full of weeping than you can understand.'
>
> 'THE STOLEN CHILD', W. B. YEATS

Beckoning to us down the centuries is a faeryland of plenty, an earthly paradise overflowing with the most delicious fruits and fragrant flowers.

The land of heart's desire, faeryland shifts shape as swiftly and effortlessly as its resident spirits. It is at its most bewitching, however, as the garden of our dreams. An enchanted Eden, it draws us on but shuts us out.

Or does it? Tantalising legends tell of secret paths into the faery world, and as often as not the best way in has been the least expected. Some unwary travellers have simply stumbled upon it.

The Cornish farmer Mr Noy was one such unsuspecting traveller. One night, he took a short-cut across Selena Moor, and in its desolate heart he found himself in 'a most beautiful orchard'. There he met his sweetheart, Grace, whom he thought had died, but who had actually been captured by the faeries. She 'led him into a bowery walk, where all kinds of flowers were blooming'.

Grace explained how she had been out wandering when she 'got lost in a place where ferns were above her head'. She was unable to leave, because she had unwittingly eaten one of the luscious faery fruits hanging in the enchanted orchard.

Mr Noy was captivated by the glorious garden, but the brightest flower within it was Grace, and he was heartbroken when he was unable to break the spell that bound her. Ejected unceremoniously by the faeries, he spent the rest of his life pining both for his lost love and that perilous magic orchard.

When another Cornish inhabitant, Cherry of Zennor, took a walk on the wild side, it was also a ravishing but heart-wrenching experience. Cherry had been hired as a home help by a handsome gentleman, who turned out to be a faery. He took her on a long and winding journey:

> 'They went an immense way down and down twisting lanes with high hedges closing above them. The gentleman lifted Cherry over several streams and at length they came to a gate into a garden where flowers of all seasons grew and flowered together. Birds were singing all round them, and Cherry thought she had never seen so lovely a place.'

Cherry fell in love with her mystery employer as they cultivated his beautiful garden; they would kiss each other at the end of every row. She would have stayed there for ever.

But it was not to be. When Cherry let slip that she knew her lover was a faery, he cast her out.

Visits to the faery garden have been described throughout the centuries. One of the most recent experiences involved two men on a hunting trip on a cold and snowy day in New York state in 1962. One of the hunters, Patrick Arnone, noticed a tall stand of pines and thought it would be the perfect place to find deer. On exploring further, Mr Arnone was amazed by what lay beyond the pines: 'I groped through another wall of underbrush, this one green and flowering, and entered an area of about three to five acres of green grass, flowers, with birds singing and squirrels chattering. The temperature was near 80 degrees. Impossible, I thought.'

The two men sunbathed for a while and then returned home. Alas, when they tried to retrace their footsteps on a later occasion, the faery garden had simply vanished.

TREE MAGIC

Towering above us, the tree was the first plant to be worshipped by mankind. Growing stronger, wider and higher as the years rolled by, it symbolised strength, fertility, and even everlasting life.

The greatest of the magic trees was Yggdrasill from Norse mythology. A vast evergreen ash, it overshadowed the whole universe. Rooted in Asgard, the enchanted mountain meeting place of the gods, Yggdrasill's leaves were the clouds and its fruits were the stars.

In folklore the ash is one of a magic trilogy of trees that usually marks the entrance to the faery garden. Wherever the ash, oak and thorn grow together, it is said, there will the faeries gather. Enter the space between two oaks within that magic grove, and you will be in faeryland.

Faeries can often be found within the trees. Like the wood nymphs of classical mythology, the tree elves of folklore are the guardians of the woods and wild animals. Magical shape-shifters, they may manifest themselves as the tree itself, or as tiny beings living inside it.

The sacred oak worshipped by the Druids has always had a powerful attraction for the faeries, as the old proverb 'fairy folks are in old oaks' makes clear. Its most sinister elf residents must be the Oakmen. Little wizened creatures, with red noses and matching caps of red toadstools, they inhabit 'thrice-cut' oak coppices, and deal severely with anyone cutting or damaging their oaks without first asking permission.

A solitary hawthorn, or a magic ring of three or more thorn trees may mark a faery hill. It was by 'the fairy thorn on the steep' that beautiful young Anna Grace was stolen away by the faeries, according to Samuel Ferguson's mournful nineteenth-century ballad 'The Fairy Thorn'. Alas, Anna Grace and three girlfriends strayed too close to the faery tree one night and they were spellbound:

> 'For, from the air above, and the grassy ground beneath,
> And from the mountain-ashes and the old Whitethorn between,
> A Power of faint enchantment doth through their beings breathe,
> And they sink down together on the green.'

Lying on the cold ground, unable to move, Anna's three companions watched helplessly as their friend was abducted by 'the silent fairy crowd' that flowed down upon them 'like a river in the air'.

The thorn was still working its powerful magic in 1920, when two faery thorns growing together in a field at Kiltimagh, in Ireland, were felled to build a local hospital. The foolish woodcutter had been warned that it might be the last thing he ever did, but added insult to injury by responding: 'I'll be back, never fear, and to hell with your bloody faeries!'

The faery vengeance was swift and merciless. The woodcutter was paralysed by a stroke the same night. He returned to the town, as he had promised, but it was in a coffin a year later. The hospital was built but it never opened.

Another all-powerful magic tree is the elder. There are many cautionary tales concerning those who failed to heed warnings not to cut down or damage a faery elder.

The most famous of England's faery elders, which stands by the Rollright Stones in Oxfordshire, submitted to being pruned, but only as part of a reverential ceremony. The tree was believed to be the manifestation of a guardian faery, who looked after the surrounding countryside and had transformed a warmongering king and his invading army into the ancient standing stones in order to protect the local people.

A celebratory Midsummer Eve feast was held annually at the 'King' stone to mark the event, after which the elder was ceremonially cut. Miraculously, the tree bled and its blood brought fertility to the land.

Many tree nuts and cones also possess the magic power to confer fertility. A wedding present of a bag of hazelnuts to a bride is believed to increase her chances of conceiving. Carrying a walnut around in its shell is a possible remedy for infertility. The most effective magical aid, however, must be the acorn, which can be worn not only to help conceive and to promote sexual relations, but also to preserve youthfulness. Pine cones can also be carried around as fertility charms.

The Little Elder Tree Mother

Thanks to the magical Elder Tree Mother, a little boy enjoys an enchanted ride through the seasons in this extract from a fairy tale written by Hans Christian Andersen in 1845.

And then she took the little boy and placed him on her bosom. The elder branches, full of blossoms, closed over them and it was as if they sat in a thick leafy bower, which flew with them through the air. It was beautiful beyond all description.

The Elder Tree Mother had suddenly become a charming young girl but her dress was still of the same green material, covered with white blossoms, as the Elder Tree Mother had worn. She had real elder blossom on her bosom, and a wreath of the same flowers was wound round her curly golden hair. Her eyes were so large and blue it was wonderful to look at them.

She and the boy kissed each other, and then they were of the same age and felt the same joys. They walked hand in hand out of the bower, and now stood at home in a beautiful flower garden.

Near the green lawn the father's walking stick was tied to a post. There was life in this stick, for as soon as they seated themselves upon it, the polished knob turned into a neighing horse's head, a long black mane was fluttering in the wind, and four strong slender legs grew out of it.

The little girl seized the boy round the waist, and they flew far into the country. It was Spring and it became Summer, it was Autumn and it became Winter, and thousands of pictures reflected themselves in the boy's eyes and heart, and the little girl always sang again: "You will never forget that!" And during their whole flight, the elder tree smelled so sweetly.

"It's beautiful here in the Spring," said the little girl, and they were again in the green beech wood, where the thyme breathed forth sweet fragrance at their feet, and the pink anemones looked lovely in the green moss. "Here it is splendid in Summer!" she said, and they passed by old castles of the age of chivalry. The high walls and the battlements were reflected in the water of the ditches, on which swans were swimming. The corn waved in the field like a yellow sea. Red and yellow flowers grew in the ditches, wild hops and convolvuli were in full bloom in the hedges. In the evening, the moon rose, large and round, and the hayricks in the meadows smelt sweetly. "One can never forget it!"

"Here it is beautiful in Autumn," said the little girl, and the atmosphere seemed twice as high and blue, while the wood shone with crimson, green and gold. The hounds were running off, flocks of wild fowl flew screaming over the barrows, while the bramble bushes twined round the old stones. The dark blue sea was covered with white sailing ships, and in the barns sat old women, girls and children picking hops into a large tub. The young ones sang songs and the old people told fairy tales about goblins and sorcerers.

It could not be more pleasant anywhere.

"Here it's agreeable in Winter!" said the little girl, and all the trees were covered with hoar frost, so that they looked like white coral. The snow creaked under one's foot, as if one had new boots on. One shooting star after another traversed the sky. In the room, the Christmas tree was lit, and there were songs and merriment. In the peasant's cottage, the violin sounded, and games were played for apple quarters. Even the poorest child said: "It is beautiful in Winter!"

And indeed it was beautiful! And the little girl showed everything to the boy, and the elder tree continued to breathe forth sweet perfume.

At parting, the little girl took an elder blossom from her breast and gave it to him as a keepsake. He placed it in his prayer-book and when he opened it in distant lands, it was

always at the place where the flower of remembrance was lying. And the more he looked at it the fresher it became, so that he could almost smell the fragrance of the woods at home. He distinctly saw the little girl, with her bright blue eyes, peeping out from behind the petals, and heard her whispering: "Here it is beautiful in Spring, in Summer, in Autumn and in Winter", and hundreds of pictures passed through his mind.'

Under the Green Hill

> 'Lay your ear close to the hill.
> Do you not catch the tiny clamour,
> Busy click of an elfin hammer.'
> 'THE LEPRACAUN',
> WILLIAM ALLINGHAM

Be sure to take care when passing an ancient burial mound, for the grassy barrow, or hollow hill, is a favourite haunt of the faeries, as many an unwary traveller has discovered.

Ancient hilltop earth forts are one of the many secret entrances to a faery garden. On a magic summer evening, a host of faeries are more than likely to stream out of those enchanted portals for a wild night of dancing on their green front lawns.

A 'rather lofty hill' in Midridge, County Durham, features in many tales as a great place for faery sightings. A glimpse of just one of the faery dancers who issued forth from the hill on midsummer evenings was eagerly sought by local lovers. It was believed that any man or woman who saw a faery reveller would soon wed the love of their life. As in all faery encounters, due respect had to be observed. Visitors should come singly and they should never address the faeries directly.

A local lad named Willy ignored the rules and suffered the consequences. One night in August, after a heavy drinking session to celebrate the safe gathering of the harvest, he was foolish enough to ride out to the bottom of the hill and shout to the faeries to come out:

'Scarcely had the last words escaped his lips ere he was nearly surrounded by many hundreds of the little folks, who are ever ready to revenge, with the infliction of the most dreadful punishment, every attempt at insult.'

Scared out of his wits, Willy galloped to the nearest house. He just managed to get inside and shut out the angry pursuing faeries. When it was safe to venture out, he found that he had narrowly missed death by javelin. The lethal weapon hurled by the faery king was still sticking out of the armour-plated front door.

The secret entrance could be a steep climb up a high mountain. In one Irish legend a 'half-fool' piper was invited to play at a great feast in a faery palace at the summit of Croagh Patric, in Galway. He was guided there by a Puca, who 'rushed him across hills and bogs and rough places, till he brought him to the top of Croagh Patric. Then the Puca struck three blows with his foot, and a great door opened and they passed in together, into a fine room.'

The hidden opening to a wilderness faery garden was memorably described by the seventeenth-century English poet William Browne in 'Britannia's Pastorals':

'An arched cave cut in a rock entire,
Deep, hollow, hideous, o'ergrown with grass,
With thorns and briers, and sad mandragora.'

The mandragora, or magic mandrake plant, growing there was a vital clue to what lay beyond.

A first-hand description of what lies within a faery cavern was provided in the Middle Ages by the two 'Green Children', who were discovered lying by the mouth of a pit in Suffolk. The green-skinned brother and sister were cared for by locals and believed to be faeries. Asked to describe her homeland, the girl said that they 'saw no sun, but enjoyed a degree of light like what is after sunset'. She and her brother had wandered out of this land, she explained, while they were herding sheep.

'We came to a certain cavern,' she recalled, 'on entering which we heard a delightful sound of bells; ravished by whose sweetness, we went for a long time wandering on through the cavern until we came to its mouth. When we came out of it, we were struck senseless by the excessive light of the sun, and the unusual temperature of the air; and thus we lay for a long time. Being terrified by the noise of those who came on us, we wished to fly, but we could not find the entrance of the cavern before we were caught.'

Deep Water

The faery garden may be many fathoms deep. A fortunate few have glimpsed the watery home of the faeries of Lough Neagh in Ireland. The Welsh topographer Giraldus Cambrensis first spotted their faery palaces in the twelfth century, when the tops of the towers, 'built after the fashion of the country', were visible in calm, clear water under the surface of the lake.

More evidence of underwater faery activity was recorded in the nineteenth century, when folklorist Lady Wilde noted that boatmen crossing Lough Neagh late at night 'have often heard sweet music rising up from beneath the waves and the sound of laughter, and seen glimmering lights far down under the water, where the ancient fairy palaces are supposed to be'.

Further south, the Lake of Killarney was once the scene of an astonishing faery commotion, according to folk legend. An ancient chieftain named O'Donoghue was believed to inhabit the lough in spirit form, and to manifest himself annually on May Day morning:

'The first beams of the rising sun were just gilding the lofty summit of Glena, when the waters near the eastern shore of the lake became suddenly and violently agitated, though all the rest of the surface lay smooth and still ... a foaming wave darted forward. Behind this wave appeared a stately warrior fully armed, mounted upon a milk white steed. The warrior was O'Donoghue, followed by numberless youths and maidens linked together by garlands of delicious Spring flowers, and they timed their movements to strains of enchanting melody.'

Lake spirits are more frequently apparitions of beautiful women, notably the fabled Welsh water faeries, the Gwragedd Annwn. In the twelfth century, it is said, a Welsh lake maiden left her underwater faery palace to marry a local farmer. She bore her husband three children, but when he ignored her father's warning never to give her 'three causeless blows', she promptly vanished back into the lake, taking her priceless dowry of magic cattle with never-ending milk.

Beautiful faery maidens have also been known to emerge from the wells they guard. Pilgrims to the Celtic Well of the Triple Goddess on the Isle of Sheppey in Kent, have reported seeing a ghostly lady dressed in white, and of smelling a strong scent of flowers as they leave their votive offerings.

Water faeries can manifest themselves in far more unpleasant forms, however, and frequently do. The kelpie, for example, enjoys lurking in rivers and leaping out to terrorise unsuspecting travellers. It can also transform itself into a young horse and gallop away with anyone foolish enough to mount it. It will then throw its rider into the nearest deep pool and disappear in a flash of light.

The most popular haunt of the water faeries, however, is the wide and fathomless ocean. The home of a multitude of different magical beings, its best-known resident must be the mermaid. A beautiful woman with the tail of a fish, the mermaid is the ultimate *femme fatale* and the spirit personification of the sea at its most seductive and deadly.

The most famous sea faery of all is Hans Christian Andersen's Little Mermaid, who lost her heart to a mortal prince. Her underwater palace had its own faery garden – a magic meadow full of bright red and dark blue flowers growing among flame-like blossoms and glittering gold fruit. The Little Mermaid also culti-vated an extraordinary garden of her own, in which she planted a single tree. She chose a willow, revered as 'The Tree of Enchantment' in folklore. It was placed next to a shipwrecked marble statue of a handsome youth, which helped inspire her ill-fated romance:

'It grew splendidly, and very soon hung its fresh branches over the statue, almost down to the blue sands. The shadow had a violet tint, and waved to and fro like the branches; it seemed as if the crown of the tree and the root were at play, and trying to kiss each other.'

Dangerous Crossings

There are many pitfalls in the faery garden, as the cautionary tales of solitary travellers who have been 'pixy-led' and lost their way in lonely places in the dead of night testify.

The antisocial faeries who haunted the Lincolnshire fens, for example, liked to terrify local people travelling after dark by shouting out to them in the same voices as loved ones who had died. Anyone forced to go out into the fens at night would carry a protective charm, such as a bible-ball – a page from the bible crumpled up into a tight ball – in the hope of a safe crossing.

The most famous fen faery was known as Tiddy Mun. He was a guardian spirit who lurked in deep water holes and prevented local homes from being flooded during heavy rain, but he turned nasty in the seventeenth century, when a group of Dutchmen started draining his watery home for agricultural projects.

When the water started draining away, Tiddy Mun grew angry. At first, the Dutchmen who had been brought in to do the work bore the brunt of his rage. He lured them into dangerous bog holes, where they drowned. But when the work continued, he turned on the local people and caused their babies and livestock to die, and their houses to fall down.

Fortunately for the fen people, they were able to placate the angry faery. They all gathered by a dyke on the night of a new moon and each person ceremonially emptied fresh water into it, while chanting:

'Tiddy Mun, wi-out a name,
Here's watter for thee, tak' tha
spell undone!'

There was a great wailing noise, and when it died down they heard the pewits call 'low and sweet' and they knew Tiddy Mun had forgiven them. Just to be sure, however, they carried out the same ritual each month.

The flickering lights created by the spontaneous ignition of marsh gases inspired the popular notion of mischievous faeries using lanterns to lead unwary travellers into ditches and bogs. Sometimes the 'pixy-leading' was a faery punishment for wrongdoing, as in the case of 'old toad' Farmer Mole. Disgusted by the West Country farmer's drunken habit of beating his wife and children, the pixies decided to teach him a permanent lesson one evening when he was riding home across a lonely part of the moor.

'This foggy night the old veller were wicked drunk and a-waving his gad and reckoning how he'd drub his Missus when he zee a light in the mist.' The pony he was riding was sober enough to see it was a pixy holding a lantern, and refused to go any further. Farmer Mole staggered towards the light on foot and was sucked down forever into 'the blackest, deepest bog' on the moor.

An attempt at 'pixy-leading' was reported in 1961 by the president of a West Country branch of the Women's Institute, who had asked for directions at a remote farm to a nearby manor house. 'I was to cross certain fields, and to go down a certain track to where there were two gates, and I must take the white one,' she recalled. 'I came to a gate at the end, set in a thick hawthorn hedge, one gate, and it wasn't white and I had a most creepy feeling.' Who knows what would have happened if

she had gone through the phantom gate? Fortunately, a farm lad sent to make sure she didn't get lost arrived at that moment, whereupon the hedge vanished and the white gate suddenly appeared. 'The old manor house was there, right in front of me, and I went in at a run,' she said.

Crossing the faery garden could be dangerous for travellers, but building a house across a faery track could also spell disaster. It was well known that no one living inside such a dwelling would ever prosper.

Such paths often followed original ley lines, as was the case at Godshill on the Isle of Wight, where a project to build a church sparked some extraordinary events. The proposed site was marked out with stones, but that night the markers were magically relocated to the top of the hill. The local bishop ordered the markers to be restored to their original positions, but at midnight they were seen rolling of their own volition back up the hill. Wisely, he decided to build the church on the hill, where it still stands.

Lost in the Mist

This cautionary tale from the Scottish Highlands was part of a collection by the nineteenth-century folklorist Thomas Keightley. It warns of the dangers of following the wrong kind of light in the fog of the importance of remembering to use protective magic charms. It also demonstrates what angry faeries are capable of if thwarted. These particular faeries were already holding a mortal woman captive and their target in this story was lucky to escape alive. The faeries used their magic, however, to steal away his unprotected property and to leave worthless substitutes in its place. These magic substitutes, which looked identical to the real thing, were called 'stocks'.

While searching one day for his goats on a hill, the tenant of the farm of Auchriachan in Strathavon, found himself suddenly enveloped in a dense fog. The thick mist persisted until night fell and he began to despair of finding his way home. But suddenly he beheld a glimmering light at no great distance.

Dancing before him, it beckoned him on. He hastened towards it and found that it proceeded from a strange-looking edifice. The door was open and he entered in. Great was his surprise when he met a woman whose funeral he had lately attended. She told him that this was an abode of the faeries, for whom she kept house. She warned him that his only chance of getting out again safely was to conceal himself from them, and she hid him in a dark corner of the apartment.

Presently, in came a troop of faeries and they all began calling out for food. An old dry-looking fellow among them then reminded them of the miserly – as it called him – tenant of Auchriachan, and how he had cheated the faeries out of their lawful share of his property by using some magic charms taught him by his old grandmother.

"The tenant of Auchriachan is now away from his home," said the faery. "He is searching for our allies, his goats. While he is gone, his family have neglected to use the magic charm to protect his animals. So, let us eat his favourite ox for supper."

The speaker was Thomas the Rhymer, who lived with the queen of Elfland for seven years. And his plan was adopted with acclamation.

"But what are we to do for bread?" cried one faery.

"We'll have Auchriachan's new-baked bread," replied Thomas. "His wife forgot to put a magic cross on the first bannock."

No sooner was it said than it was done. The ox was brought in and slaughtered before the very eyes of its master, who was hidden in the corner. But while the faeries were employed about their cooking, the woman gave him an opportunity for escape.

The dense fog had now cleared away and the moon was shining bright. The tenant of Auchriachan, therefore, was soon able to reach his home. His wife instantly produced a basket of new-baked bannocks with milk, and she urged him to eat. Her husband's mind was on his ox, however, and he asked his family who had fed the cattle that night. His eldest son told the tenant that it was him.

"Did you use the charm?" entreated his father.

"I forgot," confessed the son.

"Alas! Alas!" moaned his father. "My favourite ox is no more!"

"How can that be?" said his son. "I saw the ox alive and well not two hours ago."

"It was nothing but fairy stock," cried his father. "Bring the ox out here and I'll show you."

The faery ox was led forth, and the tenant of Auchriachan abused it and those that substituted it for his own ox with angry words. Then he felled the ox. He flung the carcase down the brae at the back of the farmhouse, and he hurled the faery bread after it. There they both lay untouched – for it was observed with wonder that neither cat nor dog would put a tooth in either of them.'

A Miniature Paradise

> '*I know a bank where the wild thyme blows,*
> *Where oxlips and the nodding violet grows,*
> *Quite over-canopied with luscious woodbine,*
> *With sweet musk roses, and with eglantine;*
> *There sleeps Titania sometime of the night,*
> *Lull'd in these flowers with dances and delight.*'

he faery queen Titania's flowery bower, described so
evocatively by Shakespeare in *A Midsummer Night's Dream*, was a mini paradise in the heart of the English countryside, and it completely changed the way people imagined faeryland.

The rich trappings of Titania's fairy court were provided by a heady bouquet of familiar flowers, but the freshness of Shakespeare's perspective gave them an enduring appeal. In his miniature faery kingdom, the plants loomed so large they gained a new magnificence. Described from the view-point of a tiny faery, the flowers that had been taken for granted emerged transformed, as the jewels in her crown.

In this strange and beautiful new world, cowslips became royal courtiers. Their 'gold coats' were speckled with rubies and their pearl earrings were dewdrops. Faeries dined off honey-bags stolen from the bees, and fanned their queen with 'the wings from painted butterflies'.

The novelty of Shakespeare's decorative faeryland captured the popular imagination, and seventeenth-century British poets vied with one another to create yet more elaborate and fanciful miniature worlds.

The height of diminutive elegance, the faery king, Oberon, in a poem by Sir Simeon Steward, sports a belt 'made of Mirtle leaves/Pleyted in small curious theaves/Besett with Amber Cowslipp studdes/And fring'd a bout with daysie budds'. In Robert Herrick's equally whimsical profile of the faery king, 'Oberon's Feast', the tiny monarch feasts on 'horns of papery butterflies', washed down with a little 'cuckoo's spittle'.

Poets have continued to delight in revealing magical miniature worlds within the countryside. The nineteenth-century English poet William Allingham penned 'A Forest in Fairyland', glowingly illustrated by Richard Doyle and loosely inspired by Shakespeare's 'magical wood'. Allingham's faeries are so minuscule that a convoy is needed to bear the weight of a single flower, as he makes clear in this description of a lovelorn faery's gift to his sweetheart:

> 'He sends her bossy peonies,
> Fat as himself. So please her eyes,
> And double-poppies, mock flow'rs made
> In clumsy gold, for brag display'd;
> Ten of the broadest-shoulder'd elves
> To carry one must strain themselves.'

The Midnight Garden

while you make the sign of the cross and similarly anoint yourself. You should then stroke the cat's tail three times over your left eye, then your right eye, saying:

> *'Elves of the night, enchant my sight,*
> *Your forms for to see in moon and sunlight;*
> *With this spell and with this sign*
> *I pri'thee, forward my design.'*

A useful precaution to take, according to legend, in case the faeries you encounter turn nasty, would be to arm yourself with a four-leafed clover. Such a ploy was used to successful effect by the heroine of a nineteenth-century English faery story by J. H. Hewing, who was captured by the faeries but managed to escape while they were dancing by wishing upon a four-leafed clover.

Different phases of the moon create their own magic. It is advisable to use the light of the waxing moon to plant flowers both to attract faeries to your garden and to use to cast your own spells. When the waxing crescent appears in the evening sky, it is the best time to plant in order to ensure a fruitful crop. The arrival of the full moon is accompanied by a surge of magical power that generally signals the coming of the faeries. The waning moon is the most auspicious time to banish them. In the dark of the moon, no magic should be attempted.

Seize the right moment, for if the breeze is right, you could 'sail away to Fairyland, Along this track of light.'

> *'By the moone we sport and play,*
> *With the night begins our day;*
> *As we daunce, the deaw doth fall.'*
> 'BY THE MOONE', THOMAS RAVENSCROFT

Moon magic is a powerful enchantment. Venture out of doors when others lie in bed and you may be rewarded with a glimpse of faeries dancing on a smooth green lawn, within a dark wood, or upon a lonely heath.

Faery time is night time, and folk legend is full of surprise sightings of faery revellers dancing their magic rounds by the light of the moon. 'I have never seen a man faery or a woman faery,' commences one nineteenth-century Scottish story, 'but my mother saw a troop of them. She herself and other maidens of the town were milking cows in the evening gloaming, when they observed a flock of faeries, reeling and setting upon the green plain in front of the knell.'

If you are not fortunate enough to stumble across a secret faery gathering, you can cast your own spell to make such magic meetings visible. For the magic to work, you must step out into your garden with a female black cat during an evening when the Northern Lights are in the sky. The cat must be stroked until she purrs contentedly and when she stretches for the first time, she should be anointed with wine

Etheline E Dall

Living off the Land

Within the abundant faery garden, trees always hang heavy with forbidden fruit. Too often, the temptation to taste is irresistible, and the dreadful consequences are always immediate: 'Eating a tempting plum in this enchanted orchard was my undoing,' the Cornish farmer Mr Noy is warned by his sweetheart Grace, when he is reunited with her in a magic orchard.

As Grace relates in the Cornish tale, she 'came to an orchard where music was sounding', but although the music was sometimes quite near, she could not get out of the orchard, and wandered around as if she was pixy-led.

At length, worn out with hunger and thirst, she plucked a beautiful golden plum from one of the trees and began to eat it. It dissolved into bitter water in her mouth, and she fell to the ground in a faint. When she revived, she found herself surrounded by a crowd of little people, who laughed and rejoiced at getting a girl to bake and brew for them, and to look after their mortal babies.

It was painfully evident from the earliest times that produce from the faery garden should be resisted. When the seventh-century Welsh saint Collen accepted an invitation to visit a faery king, who lived at Glastonbury Tor in Somerset, he went prepared, hiding a bottle of holy water under his cassock. He entered 'the most beautiful castle that the mind of man could conceive' and was conducted to the banqueting hall, where the faery king pressed him to sit down and eat.

Unlike lesser mortals, however, eagle-eyed St Collen could see through the powerful spells transforming the food, and was brave enough to say so: 'I do not eat the leaves of a tree,' he told his host, and tipped his holy water over the faeries. They vanished and he found himself standing alone on the summit of Glastonbury Tor.

Unfortunately for Hansel and Gretel, the two lost children in the haunting fairy tale by Jacob and Wilhelm Grimm, they did not recognise the powerful magic at work when they came upon an edible cottage deep in the forest. They had been trying unsuccessfully for three days to find their way out of the enchanted wood, and they were starving.

'We will go in there,' said Hansel, 'and have a glorious feast. I will eat a piece of the roof, and you can eat the window. Will they not be sweet?'

The children discovered, too late, that the tasty cottage was an evil trick employed by a wicked faery to entice her prey inside to be fattened up and eaten. It was a story with a happy ending, however, and they managed to outwit their jailor and find their way back home.

Experts agree that it is perilous to consume faery produce, but they are undecided as to whether the faeries themselves need to eat and drink. A seventeenth-century Scottish pastor, Reverend Robert Kirk, had definite views on the subject. He believed that some were 'so spungious, thin and desecat, that they are fed only by sucking into some fine spirituous Liquors, that pierce like pure Air and Oyl; others feed more gross on the Foyson or substance of Corns and Liquors, or Corne itself that grows on the Surface of the Earth, which these Fairies steal away, partly invisible, partly preying on the grain, as do Crowes and Mice.'

Kirk's claim that the faeries stole mortal food and drink for their own consumption is a widespread belief. Cunningly, the faeries conceal the thefts by subtly extracting the nutritious essence so that there is no apparent change.

Cow's milk is believed to be a great faery delicacy, and it is said that they can drain an entire herd without quenching their thirst. The twelfth-century Welsh author Giraldus Cambrensis maintained that the faeries 'ate neither flesh nor fish but lived on a milk diet, made up of messes of saffron'.

Banqueting in Miniature

Inspired by the notion of magic faery food and drink, the seventeenth-century English poet Robert Herrick imagined what exotic delicacies a small and fussy faery king might enjoy in this fanciful poem.

Oberon's Feast

A little mushroom-table spread,
  After short prayers, they set on bread,
A moon-parch'd grain of purest wheat,
With some small glitt'ring grit, to eat
His choice bits with; then in a trice
They make a feast less great than nice.
But all this while his eye is served,
We must not think his ear was sterved;
But that there was in place to stir
His spleen, the chirring grasshopper,
The merry cricket, puling fly,
The piping gnat for minstrelsy.
And now, we must imagine first,
The elves present, to quench his thirst,
A pure seed-pearl of infant dew,
Brought and besweeten'd in a blue
And pregnant violet; which done,
His kitling eyes begin to run
Quite through the table, where he spies
The horns of papery butterflies,
Of which he eats; and tastes a little
Of that we call the cuckoo's spittle;
A little fuz-ball pudding stands
By, yet not blessed by his hands,
That was too coarse; but then forthwith
He ventures boldly on the pith
Of sugar'd rush, and eats the sagge
And well-bestrutted bees' sweet bag;
Gladding his palette with some store
Of emmets' eggs; what would he more?
But beards of mice, a newt's stewed thigh,
A bloated earwig, and a fly;
With the red-capt worm that's shut

Within the concave of a nut,
Brown as his tooth. A little moth,
Late fatten'd in a piece of cloth;
With wither'd cherries, mandrakes' ears,
Moles' eyes: to these the slain stag's tears;
The unctuous dewlaps of a snail,
The broke-heart of a nightingale
O'ercome in music; with a wine
Ne'er ravish'd from the flattering vine,
But gently prest from the soft side
Of the most sweet and dainty bride,
Brought in a dainty daisy, which
He fully quaffs up, to bewitch
His blood to height; this done, commended
Grace by his priest; the feast is ended.'

Romantic notions about the kind of food and drink that might make up the miniature faery's diet have continued to inspire writers and artists ever since Shakespeare first described a tiny faery court in *A Midsummer Night's Dream*. The nineteenth-century author William Allingham elaborated on the intoxicating effect of certain drinks in the following passage from *In Fairy Land, A Series of Pictures from the Elf-World*, which was lavishly illustrated by Richard Doyle.

A Forest in Fairyland

'Where luscious dewdrops lurk,
I with fifty went to work,
Catching delicious wine that wets
The warm blue hearts of violets:
Last moon it was the hawthorn-flower,
Next moon 'twill be virgin's bower,
Moon by moon, the varied rose,
To seal in flasks for winter mirth,
When frost and darkness wrap the earth.
Which wine delights you, fay?

All those;
But none is like the Wine of Rose.
With Wine of Rose,
In midst of snows
The sunny season flows and glows!'

Up and Away

In the beginning, before they sprouted their own wings, the faeries relied on magical plants to fly about their business. A mainstay of the faery garden was ragwort, popularly known as 'Devildums' due to its astonishing powers of flight. After plucking a ragwort stem, the faery would mount it and utter the magic password for levitation. The most effective spell, according to the seventeenth-century English writer John Aubrey, was 'Horse and Hattock'.

Speed and flight were essential in Shakespeare's miniature faery world, but the tiny beings he described were still wingless and relied on outside help to become airborne. The faery spirit Ariel in *The Tempest* sucks nectar like a bee, sleeps in a cowslip flower and rides through the sky on a bat's back. The faery Queen Mab in *Romeo and Juliet*, as befits her royal status, possesses an extraordinary aerial coach:

'Drawn with a team of little atomies
Athwart men's noses as they lie asleep;
Her waggon-spokes made of long spinners' legs;
The cover, of the wings of grasshoppers;
Her traces, of the smallest spider's web;
Her collars, of the moonshine's wat'ry beams;
Her whip, of cricket's bone; the lash, of film;
Her waggoner, a small grey-coated gnat.'

It was natural enough that the small faeries so closely identified with the insect world would metamorphose into butterfly-like beings themselves. Probably the first description of the winged faery occurs in 'The Rape of the Lock', a mock-epic poem by the eighteenth-century British poet Alexander Pope. His flying faeries were a splendid sight:

'Some to the Sun their Insect-Wings unfold,
Waft on the Breeze, or sink in Clouds of Gold,
Transparent Forms, too fine for mortal Sight,
Their fluid Bodies half dissolv'd in Light.
Loose to the Wind their airy Garments flew,
Thin glitt'ring Textures of the filmy Dew;
Dipt in the richest Tincture of the Skies,
Where Light disports in ever-mingling Dyes,
While ev'ry Beam new transient Colours flings,
Colours that change whene'er they wave their Wings.'

The image of the winged spirit soon crept into children's
faery tales. In a mid-nineteenth-century version of *Jack and
the Beanstalk*, penned by British author George Cruikshank,
the traditional figure of the faery godmother is transformed
into a beautiful winged being. Cruikshank's 'little old
woman, in a cloak and hood',
familiar from folk tales, undergoes
a dramatic change as Jack
watches:

'And then, slowly, the hood, the cloak,
and gown, with the old pale face, and
brown wrinkled hands and arms, all
disappeared or melted away into the air;
and there stood before him a most
charming and graceful little lady, with
light flaxen hair, encircled by a wreath of
little tiny flowers. She had a pair of wings
like those of some beautiful butterfly, to
which her dress corresponded. In one hand she
held a thin light wand, and in her other a Bean,
speckled with bright purple and gold.'

A small faery's quest for happiness culminated in marriage
and the gift of wings in Hans Christian Andersen's popular
late-nineteenth-century children's story *Tommelise*.
Andersen's tiny heroine grew from a magic barley-corn,
gifted to a peasant couple by a grateful beggar woman,

but she was stolen away from her happy home
one night by a fat yellow frog. Tommelise then
embarked on a series of adventures as she escaped
from the clutches of one unpleasant creature after
another. Eventually she was befriended by a swallow and
flew on its back to a magic kingdom, where she met the man
of her dreams:

*'There sat a little man in the middle of the flower, as white and
transparent as if he were of glass; the most lovely crown of gold
was upon his head, and the most beautiful bright wings upon
his shoulders; and he, too, was no larger than Tommelise.'*

She was overjoyed when he asked her to marry him, and
her happiness was complete when she was presented with
an extra-special wedding gift: 'a pair of beautiful wings, of
fine white pearl, and these were fastened on Tommelise's
shoulders, and thus she also
could fly from flower to flower –
that was such a delight!'

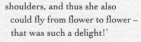

STRANGE FRUIT

Magic mushrooms must be the most potent plants in the faery garden. The poisonous nature of toadstools, or inedible mushrooms, have made them a slightly sinister addition to faeryland.

The red-and-white spotted fly agaric is the archetypal 'magic mushroom', and its hallucinatory properties have been well documented over the years. There has long been a close association between such fungi and the faeries. A pixy's preferred headgear, it was commonly believed, was a pointed mushroom-like hat.

The strange phenomenon of 'faery rings' – circles of withered or bright green grass – has also been attributed to a particular species of mushroom, which propagates by sending out a network of threads that frequently form a circular shape. According to folklore, these are the enchanted places where the faeries conduct their nightly revels.

Woe betide any mortal foolish enough to interferes with the festivities, however, as the cautionary tale of Tom, a Cornish smuggler, records. One night, Tom was dozing on the beach after a successful raid, when he was suddenly

woken by loud music. He went to investigate and was
amazed to see in the hollows between the sand banks
'glimmering lights, and persons like gaily dressed dolls
skipping about and whirling round'.

The little men he saw were dressed in green and had red
caps. The faery musicians were playing mouth organs and
whistles, and beating tambourines and cymbals. Tom
shouted at them to be quieter and instantly regretted it:

*'All the dancers, with scores and hundreds more than he noticed at
first sprang up, ranged themselves in rank and file; armed themselves
in an instant with bows and arrows, spears and slings; then faced
about, looking like vengeance. The band being disposed alongside,
played a quick march, and the troops stamped on towards Tom, who
saw them getting taller as they approached him. Their threatening
looks were so frightful that he turned tail and ran.'*

Fortunately for Tom, he was able to jump into a boat
and row out to sea before the faeries could reach him;
but he was hit by a shower of red-hot pebbles as he made
his getaway and did not dare go ashore again until it was
broad daylight.

One of the earliest faery tales, dating back to the
twelfth century, concerns the fateful allure of the faery
ring. A Shropshire nobleman, 'Wild Edric', became lost
in a forest while out hunting one night and spied 'a
large company of exceedingly beautiful ladies, taller
and larger than the human race' dancing in a circle.
Instantly smitten by the most beautiful dancer and
'forgetting the fears of enchantment, which at the first
moment had seized him', he broke into the moving circle
and captured her.

Edric was ferociously attacked 'with teeth and nails' by
the angry dancers, but escaped with his prize. He married
his beautiful faery but she was destined to break his heart.
One day she left him, never to return, and he died of sorrow.

Other plants as well as mushrooms were associated with
the faery ring, according to these verses from an eighteenth-
century play by British playwright Richard Brome:

*'At night by Moon-light on the Plain.
With Rapture, how I've seen,
Attended by her harmless Train.
The little Fairy Queen
Her midnight Revels sweetly keep
While Mortals are involved in Sleep
They tript it o'er the Green.*

*And when they danced their cheerful Round
The Morning would disclose,
For where their nimble Feet do bound,
The Daisy (fair as Maids in May),
The Cowslip in his gold Array,
And blushing Violet rose.'*

The Evil Orchard

This extract from a faery poem by nineteenth-century British writer Christina Rossetti describes the dire consequences of tasting forbidden fruit.

Goblin Market

Morning and evening
　Maids heard the goblins cry
"Come buy our orchard fruits,
Come buy, come buy.":
Evening by evening
Among the brookside rushes,
Laura bowed her head to hear,
Lizzie veiled her blushes:
Crouching close together
In the cooling weather
With clasping arms and cautioning lips,
With tingling cheeks and finger tips.
"Lie close," Laura said,
Pricking up her golden head:
"We must not look at goblin men,
We must not buy their fruits:
Who knows upon what soil they fed
Their hungry thirsty roots?"
"Come buy," call the goblins
Hobbling down the glen.
"Oh," cried Lizzie, "Laura, Laura,
You should not peep at goblin men."
Lizzie covered up her eyes,
Covered close lest they should look;
Laura raised her glossy head,
And whispered like the restless brook:
"Look, Lizzie, look Lizzie."
"No," said Lizzie: "no, no, no;
Their offers should not charm us."
She thrust a dimpled finger
In each ear, shut eyes and ran:
Curious Laura chose to linger
　Wondering at each merchant man.
　　She heard a voice like voice of doves

Cooing all together:
They sounded kind and full of love
In the pleasant weather.
Backwards up the mossy glen
Turned and trooped the goblin men,
With their shrill repeated cry,
"Come buy, come buy."
When they reached where Laura was
They stood stock still upon the moss,
Leering at each other,
Brother with queer brother;
Signalling each other,
Brother with sly brother.
Laura stared but did not stir,
Longed but had no money.
"You have much gold upon your head,"
They answered all together:
"Buy from us with a golden curl."
She clipped a precious golden lock,
Then sucked their fruit globes fair or red;
Sweeter than honey from the rock,
Stronger than man-rejoicing wine,
Clearer than water flowed that juice;
She never tasted such before,
How should it cloy with length of use?
She sucked and sucked and sucked the more
Fruits which that unknown orchard bore;
She sucked until her lips were sore.
Lizzie met her at the gate
Full of wise upbradings.
"Nay, hush," said Laura:
"Nay, hush, my sister:
I ate and ate my fill,
Yet my mouth waters still;

Tomorrow night I will
Buy more," and kissed her.
Laura turned cold as stone
To find her sister heard that cry alone.
That goblin cry
"Come buy our fruits, come buy."
Day after day, night after night,
Laura kept watch in vain

In sullen silence of exceeding pain.
She never spied the goblin men
Hawking their fruit along the glen:
But when the moon waxed bright
Her hair thin and grey;
She dwindled, as the fair full moon doth turn
To swift decay and burn
Her fire away.'

Magical Beasts

Endlessly fertile, the faery garden produced not only tempting but forbidden fruits, but also splendid magical animals. Magnificent horses were bred by the Tuatha de Danaan, the Irish faery court, as folklorist Lady Wilde noted in her nineteenth-century collection of ancient Irish legends:

> 'And the breed of horses they reared could not be surpassed in the world — fleet as the wind, with the arched neck and the broad chest and the quivering nostril, and the large eye that showed they were made of fire and flame, and not a dull, heavy earth. And the Tuatha made stables for them in the great caves of the hills, and they were shod with silver and had golden bridles, and never a slave was allowed to ride them.
> A splendid sight was the cavalcade of the Tuatha de Danaan knights. Seven-score steeds, each with a jewel on his forehead like a star, and seven score horsemen, all the sons of kings, in their green mantles fringed with gold, and golden helmets on their head, and golden greaves on their limbs, and each knight having in his hand a golden spear.'

Each faery court, however, boasted the best magical steeds; splendid horses were a highlight of the solemn rides and processions that were a favourite faery pastime. One such ride was described by two girls, who had hidden and watched, in a nineteenth-century collection of Scottish folk tales:

> 'We heard the loud laugh o' fowk riding, wi' the jingling o' bridles, and the clanking o' hoofs. We cowered down till they passed by. A leam o' light was dancing owre them, maire bonnie than moon-shine: they were a wee, wee fowk, wi' green scarfs on, but ane that rade formost, and that ane was a good deal langer than the lave, wi' bonnie lang hair bun' about wi' a strap, whilk glented lyke stars. They rade on braw wee whyte naigs, wi' unco lang swooping tails, an' manes hung wi' whustles that the win' played on. This, an' their tongues whan they sang, was like the soun' o' a far awa Psalm.'

The girls saw the faeries leap a high hawthorn hedge 'like sparrows' on their magical steeds and then gallop through a field of corn to a green hill beyond. When they returned the following morning, expecting to see the crop trampled, they were amazed to find that not 'a hoof mark was there nor a blade broken'.

According to the traditional Scottish ballad 'Young Tam Lin', faery horses came in different colours, but white was considered the most noble. When Tam Lin is captured by the faery queen, he tells his mortal sweetheart that her only chance of getting him back is to pull him from his magic steed when he rides out with the royal court on Halloween, but he warns that she must be sure to pick the right horse:

> 'O first let pass the black, lady,
> And syne let pass the brown,
> But quickly run to the milk-white steed,
> Pu ye his rider down.
>
> For I'll ride on the milk-white steed,
> And ay nearest the town;
> Because I was an earthly knight
> They gie me that renown.'

Faery cattle were also far superior to their earthly counter-parts, as folk legend testifies. Occasionally the faeries would reward a deserving farmer by adding a magical bull to his herd to improve the breeding stock and ensure plentiful milk. The elf-bull was described as smaller than an earthly bull, mouse-coloured with crop ears and short horns. It had sleek and glittering fur like an otter, and was supernaturally strong and active. The faery bull always stayed close to river banks and its favourite food was green corn.

A Scottish tale describes one fortunate farmer whose cow, 'Hawkie', was allowed to breed regularly with an elf-bull, and produced a succession of superlative calves. The farmer failed to appreciate his good fortune, however, and 'Hawkie' and her offspring abandoned him for a better life in the faery garden.

FLOWER FAERIES

The faeries have enjoyed a long and protective association with nature in their role as guardian spirits of many of our trees and plants. They also possessed great gardening skills and their fabulous gardens are frequently described in folklore.

In the Cornish legend of Cherry of Zennor, a young mortal woman entered faeryland and fell in love with her green-fingered faery employer. She was entranced by his beautiful garden 'where flowers of all seasons grew and flowered together', and enjoyed helping him to cultivate his plot.

Folklore makes clear that the faeries had a keen appreciation of flowers, which extended to mortal gardens, too. In another West Country story, an old woman successfully cultivated such a beautiful bed of tulips that the faeries used it as a night nursery for their babies:

'The pixies so delighted in this spot, that they would carry their elfin babies thither and sing them to rest. Often at the dead hour of the night a sweet lullaby was heard, and strains of the most melodious music would float in the air, that seemed to owe their origin to no other musicians than the beautiful tulips themselves; and whilst these delicate flowers waved their heads to the evening breeze, it sometimes seemed as if they were marking time to their own singing.'

Thanks to their magical visitors, the tulips always flowered for much longer than any other plant in the garden, and they also 'became as fragrant as roses'. Delighted by her prize blooms, the grateful old woman never picked a single tulip and she and the faeries lived together in harmony. When she died, however, her heir dug up the tulips and planted a parsley bed. The angry faeries responded by turning the entire garden into a barren wasteland. They continued to honour the memory of the old woman by beautifying her grave, where 'the prettiest flowers would spring up without sowing or planting'.

Shakespeare's delightful miniature faery court is enriched by its decorative association with the wild flowers growing in the magical wood of *A Midsummer Night's Dream*. Plants such as the cowslip provided the sumptuous trappings of the court: 'In their gold coats spots you see; Those be rubies, fairy favours'.

Subsequent writers and artists enjoyed elaborating on the idea, and in many accounts the faeries became even more closely involved with the surrounding vegetation.

The 'grass-green silk' and 'velvet fyne' worn by the queen of Elfland in the ancient ballad of 'Thomas the Rhymer', was exchanged for more organic garments created from leaves and flowers from Shakespeare's time onwards.

The seventeenth-century British poet Sir Simeon Steward described his miniature King Oberon as a flower faery, dressed in clothes made of flowers, including cowslips and daisies. Two centuries later, such attire had clearly become the norm. A faery soldier imagined by the British poet George Darley wears bark and leaves to go to war:

'His tough spear of a wild oat made,
His good sword of a grassy blade,
His buckram suit of shining laurel,
His shield of bark, emboss'd with coral.'

It was popularly believed that a tiny faery called a Pillywiggin nestled at the heart of flower heads so small that only a honey bee could enter them. These magical flowers were thought to include the bluebell, the cowslip, the foxglove and wild thyme growing at the base of an oak tree.

Enter the Gnome

The faery garden was not always beautiful – and neither were its occupants. Deep underground, in dark caves, there lurked a race of dwarfish magical beings who wielded powerful magic. The sixteenth-century Swiss doctor Paracelsus described the 'mountain gnomes' as earth spirits:

'The earth is like their air and acts as their vital element, for each thing exists in its vital element. Thus the earth is nothing other than the vital element of the mountain dwarves since, like spirits, they can pass through solid walls, rocks and stones.'

According to Paracelsus, the gnomes were the custodians of buried treasure. Their role as guardians of nature was to keep watch over the rich subterranean seams of gold and jewels and to make sure they remained hidden 'from our view ... so that they should not be discovered all at once, but one by one and little by little, now in one country, now in another. Thus do the mines change place with time and from one country to another, in chronological order from the first day to the last.'

Legend has it that Herla, king of the Ancient Britons, not only met a dwarf-like king of the mountain gnomes, but actually spent three centuries in his subterranean domain. The gnome king was guest of honour at Herla's wedding, for which he supplied a small army of waiters, who served delicious never-ending refreshments in 'vessels made out of precious stones, all new and wondrously wrought'. Herla was guest of honour at the faery king's own wedding a year later, and was guided deep underground for the occasion:

'They entered a cave in a very high cliff, and after some journeying through the dark, which appeared to be lighted, not by the sun or moon, but by numerous torches, they arrived at the dwarf's palace, a splendid mansion.'

Time had no meaning in that enchanted world. Herla believed that the wedding celebrations had lasted three days, and was amazed to discover on his return that he had been away for three hundred years.

Gnomes have continued to feature in folklore. Cornish gnomes, known as 'Knockers', have traditionally helped tin miners, and got their name from their generous habit of knocking to indicate where a rich seam of ore could be found. The Knockers worked their own mines with great success and forged splendid treasures, a talent shared with the ancient Nibelungen, the gnomish goldsmiths of German myth, who inspired Richard Wagner's great operatic work, *The Ring Cycle*.

The Nibelungen were spawned 'from the womb of Night and Death', and lived in the gloomy subterranean clefts and caverns of Nibelheim. Creatures of the darkness, they burrowed through the bowels of the earth, like 'worms in a dead body' and mined the metals they found there. One of their number, Alberich, discovered 'pure and noble' Rhinegold, and created a magic ring that was so powerful it made him king of the Nibelungen. He forced his faery people to work for him alone and amassed a priceless hoard of treasures, including a magic helmet, forged by his brother, which enabled its wearer to shape-shift at will.

The gnome has remained a popular but far less fearsome faery figure in Germany. It is probably best known now in sculpture form, as a decorative addition to the garden, either freestanding or perched on a toadstool. The first clay figure was made in Germany in the nineteenth century. The garden gnome was believed to bring good luck to the household and it swiftly became a popular addition. Mass-production commenced in Germany in 1872, and the garden gnome has now achieved cult status.

Caught on Camera

Many claim to have seen faeries at the bottom of their garden, but two girls living in an English village went one step further in 1917, and claimed they had photographs to prove it.

The celebrated case of the Cottingley faery photographs caused a furore when it became known in 1920, and it has continued to fascinate subsequent generations, largely because the perpetrators of the famous hoax – Elsie Wright and Frances Griffiths – managed to fool no less a person than Sir Arthur Conan Doyle, creator of the master detective Sherlock Holmes.

Most people now agree that the photographs taken by the girls of faery figures cavorting in Cottingley Glen, close to Elsie's home, are simply artful fakes created with the aid of painted cardboard cutouts. It was not until 1983, however, that the photographers confessed that this was exactly what they had done, although they continued to insist that they had indeed played with faeries in the glen as children.

When two of the five Cottingley photographs were first published in the high-circulation *Strand* magazine at Christmas in 1920, they caused an uproar because their authenticity was defended by Doyle. His extraordinary article, co-written with Edward Gardner, an experienced investigator of the paranormal, was published under the sensational headline 'Epoch-making Event – Fairies Photographed'. The entire issue was sold out

in three days and the story was taken up by newspapers around the world.

Doyle was already an enthusiastic supporter of the Spiritualist movement, and he saw the photographs as evidence that 'matter as we have known it is not really the limit of our existence'. Mr Gardner supplied the girls with twenty-four photographic plates and asked if they could take any more. They duly obliged and three more images – also authenticated by Doyle – were published in the same magazine. Doyle also defended the Cottingley faery photographs in his book *The Coming of the Fairies*, published in 1922.

By then the Cottingley 'faery' glen was attracting visitors from far and wide, eager to meet the captivating magical beings that apparently frequented the local beauty spot. Many left convinced that they had indeed seen the faeries. The clairvoyant Geoffrey Hodson visited the glen with the two girls in 1921, and was thrilled when he, too, encountered the resident faeries. He recorded the remarkable experience in his book *Fairies at Work and Play*, published in 1925. Almost immediately, Mr Hodson wrote, they were 'surrounded by a dancing group of lovely female fairies'. He was riveted by the faery leader:

'A female figure, probably two feet high, surrounded by transparent flowing drapery. There is a star on her forehead, and she has large wings which glisten with pale, delicate shades, from pink to lavender…. Her hair is golden brown and unlike those of the lesser fairies, streams behind her and merges with the flowing forces of her aura.'

Part Two

A GALLERY OF
FLOWER FAERIES

'Green' magic has empowered countless spells.

The life force within our plants is a vital energy which, once harnessed,

promises to transform our lives. Every tree, flower or herb has specific

magical properties, which must be fully understood to ensure success.

Some plants have always been more potent than others, as myth and

legend record, and each part of them can be used in different ways.

Pre-eminent in the faery garden are the plants listed here.

Their bark, leaves, flowers and fruit supply the juices that conjure love,

health and happiness.

SPRING

Violet

The sweet-scented violet was born from the passion of the Greek god Zeus, wielder of thunderbolts. According to classical myth, Zeus transformed his mistress Io into a white heifer to hide her from his suspicious wife, but she wept over the coarseness of the common grass she grazed upon. Touched by Io's tears, Zeus transformed them into fragrant violets for her to feast upon:

> *'Wheresoe'r her lips she sets,*
> *Said Zeus, be breaths called violets.'*

The violet is ruled by Venus and it has long been associated with love. Shakespeare's jealous faery King Oberon casts a mischievous spell in *A Midsummer Night's Dream*, by squeezing the juice of 'love-in-idleness', the common name of the *Viola tricolor*, into the eyes of Titania, his faery queen, to make her fall in love with an ass-eared fool.

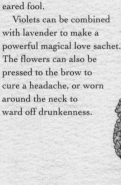

Violets can be combined with lavender to make a powerful magical love sachet. The flowers can also be pressed to the brow to cure a headache, or worn around the neck to ward off drunkenness.

Cowslip

The cowslip has bloomed in myth and religion for centuries. Its distinctive flower-head gave it the popular name of the 'Key Flower'.

In Norse mythology, the cowslip was dedicated to Freya, the goddess of sexual desire, who used it to unlock her treasure palace, and in folklore it opens the way to faery riches. Christians referred to the flower as 'Our Lady's Keys', which could unlock the Kingdom of Heaven.

The cowslip is ruled by Venus and has been dedicated to love. A popular country custom was to weave flower-heads around a roll of grass to make a fragrant yellow ball, known as a 'tosty'. The tosty was used as a love oracle to divine the identity of a future spouse. It was thrown while calling out possible names. The name uttered when caught was the lucky one.

> *'Titsy tosty, tell me true*
> *Who shall I be married to?'*

A cowslip could also be placed under the pillow to inspire a dream of love to identify a future lover. Its leaves added to a cold cream are said to preserve a youthful complexion.

Hawthorn

The powerful magical powers of the hawthorn date back to ancient Rome, where it was used as a charm against witchcraft and sorcery, and its leaves were put into the cradles of newborn babies to ward off evil spirits.

It was also regarded as a tree of great religious significance. During the first century AD, St Joseph of Arimathaea is believed to have visited the Druids at Glastonbury in Somerset. He thrust his staff into the ground and it miraculously rooted and grew into the Holy Thorn, a marvellous tree that regularly blossomed twice a year – at spring and at Christmas. Occasionally it was seen to bud, flower, berry and die all at the same time. Bad luck has always befallen anyone foolish enough to try to damage the Glastonbury Thorn, as it is known in folklore.

Strong magic – for both good and evil – also resides in hawthorn blossom. In some parts of Britain, it is believed to be very dangerous to bring May blossom into the house, and particularly to sleep with it in the same room. In other areas, however, it is welcomed indoors:

'We've been rambling all the night
And sometime of this day
And now, returning back again,
We bring a garland gay.
A garland gay we bring you here
And at your door we stand
It is a sprout well budded out
The work of our Lord's hand.'

Branches of flowering hawthorn were customarily placed in Staffordshire attics to protect the house from evil spirits.

There are also opposing views about the possible outcome of sitting under a hawthorn. For some it is something to be avoided at all costs, because witches like to dance there. For others, the shade of a hawthorn tree offers magical protection against witches.

Astrologically, the hawthorn is ruled by Mars. Its wood can also be used magically to prevent lightning strikes.

Bluebell

The first wild hyacinth, better known as bluebell, blossomed from grief. According to Greek myth, the flower was named after Hyacinth, a handsome youth beloved both by the sun god Apollo and the god of the west wind Zephyrus. Hyacinth died of a fatal wound as a result of their jealous rivalry, but the blood he shed was transformed into the flower that bears his name.

'The hyacinth bewrays the doleful "Ai",
And culls the tribute of Apollo's sigh,
Still on its bloom the mournful flower retains
The lovely blue that dyed the stripling's veins.'

In country legend bluebells are faery flowers and children were warned never to stray alone into a bluebell wood and pick one, for it would anger the faeries and the child would never find his or her way back home. A sinister alternative name for the flower was 'dead-men's bells', referring to the belief that if you hear the bluebell ring it is time for you to die.

Astrologically, the bluebell is ruled by Venus. Its flowers can be used as a magical protection to guard against nightmares. Breathing in the scent of fresh bluebells can soothe feelings of grief.

Willow

The folk name for willow is 'Tree of Enchantment'. For the ancient Sumerians it was the embodiment of the goddess of life. For the Greeks, the tree was sacred both to Hecate, the patron of magic, the sorceress Circe, and Persephone, goddess of the underworld.

The Druids discovered that willow bark contains salicin, which has analgesic properties, and it has become known as 'witches' aspirin'. The tissues of willow synthesise salicyclic acid, which is the basic ingredient of aspirin.

The willow is ruled by the moon. If planted in the garden, especially near a spring or river, it will bring the blessings of the moon to the occupant and will guard the home. Its magical properties traditionally helped witches to fly. The binding for their magic brooms is pliant willow branches, and its flexible stems are also knotted to bind their magical energy into a spell. When the wish is granted, the knot can be untied and the willow wand used again for a fresh spell.

In Christian tradition, the willow symbolised grief and was associated with Passiontide and Easter. It was also popularly identified with heartbreak. A garland of willow could be worn to signify the loss of a lover. When Shakespeare's Othello spurns his wife Desdemona, she is haunted by the image:

'The fresh streams ran by her, and murmur'd her moans;
Sing willow, willow, willow;
Her salt tears fell from her and softened the stones;
Sing willow, willow, willow,
Sing all a green willow must be my garland.'

Periwinkle

Known in the West Country as 'sorcerer's violet', the periwinkle is ruled by Venus and has long been a common ingredient of love potions.

One unsavoury love charm was to chop together powdered leaves, houseleek and earthworms. If taken by a man and woman with their meals, the potion promised to 'cause love between them'.

The periwinkle is also associated with death. If anyone was foolish enough to pluck a periwinkle growing on a grave, the occupant would rise out of it to haunt them. In the Middle Ages, garlands of periwinkle were placed on the heads of prisoners condemned to death.

A plant of magical protection, a bunch of periwinkle hung up at the threshold can ward off evil spirits. Gazing into a periwinkle flower is also believed to restore lost memory.

Herbalists advised wrapping periwinkle stems around limbs affected by cramp, as an antidote. The bruised leaves were also mixed with lard to make a soothing ointment to apply to inflamed skin or piles.

Tulip

According to Oriental legend, the tulip blossomed from the tears of a Persian youth, Ferhad, as he lay in the desert dying of a broken heart. Every tear falling into the barren sand was transformed into a beautiful tulip. Since then it has been the Oriental symbol of perfect love. It was also believed to be a lucky plant, and wearing a tulip charm traditionally promoted prosperity.

When tulips were imported to Holland in the sixteenth century, they were so popular that they were adopted as its national flower, and inspired the Tulipomania craze, at the height of which, a single bulb of the most prized variety could cost the same as a house. Ruled by Jupiter, the flamboyant tulip plays an important role in the language of flowers, in which it symbolises love, eloquence and springtime. To present a red tulip is a declaration of love. The gift of a yellow tulip signifies hopeless love, and a variegated tulip means 'your eyes are beautiful'.

In West Country legend, the faeries reportedly adopted the tulip as an ideal cradle in which to rock their babies to sleep.

Daisy

Spring has sprung, so the old adage goes, when you can cover three daisies with your foot. The generic botanical name for the daisy is *bellus*, from which it takes its dual meaning of 'pretty' (*bel*) or 'war' (*bellum*). In its battling aspect, it was recommended by herbalists as 'fitted to heal wounds in war'. An ointment prepared from crushed daisy leaves can be used to help reduce the soreness caused by bruising.

It was the wood spirit Belides, from classical myth, who gave the plant its name. She was dancing in a meadow with fellow nymphs when she was spotted by the lustful god of the orchard, Vertumnus. She was pursued by him, and transformed herself into a daisy to escape his clutches.

The classical link between the daisy and the dancing nymph was continued in folk legend. Turf trod by the

faeries during a traditional 'round' dance, was believed to sprout a ring of daisies.

The country name for the daisy, which is ruled by Venus, is 'day's eye'. It comes from the flower's habit of closing its petals at night, as the fourteenth-century British poet Geoffrey Chaucer noted in this tribute:

'Well by reason men call it maie
The Daisie, or els the Eye of the Daie.
The Empresse and floure of floures all.'

Clover

Clover is a popular symbol both of good and evil. Clover with five leaves is considered unlucky, but a four-leaf clover is a potent good-luck charm and can grant wishes. According to the old folk rhyme:

'One leaf for fame.
And one for wealth,
One for a faithful lover,
And one to bring you glorious health
Are in a four-leaf clover.'

A three-leaf clover was believed to provide magical protection. It was also used in potions to bestow youth and beauty. One magical recipe to keep looking young is to gather dew on May Day morning just before sunrise. Add three stalks of clover and let them steep in the dew in a dark place until just before sunrise the day afterwards. Rub a little of the water on your face and repeat at the same time daily for as long as your magic potion lasts. Clover is ruled by Mercury. In its three-leaf form it represents the Trinity, or the threefold aspect of life as body, soul and spirit.

Lily-of-the-Valley

This pretty plant is a formidable brain, lymph and heart herb. It has been successfully employed in treating patients recovering from strokes, especially when their speech is slow to return, and to soothe the nerves and reduce high blood pressure. A potent infusion can be made from the flowering stems.

Ruled by Mercury, in the language of flowers the lily-of-the-valley signifies the return of happiness. Its pure white flowers and bowed head have made it an emblem of chastity and humility.

According to French legend, the flowers originally sprang from the blood of St Leonard, who lived the life of a hermit in the depths of the woods. He regularly fought the dragon Temptation there, and eventually succeeded in driving the monster out of the woods until it vanished altogether. The places where the two battled were marked by beds of lily-of-the-valley.

In West Country folk tradition, however, a fresh bed of lily-of-the-valley was something to be shunned. Anyone planting one, it was said, would be dead within a year.

Summer

Foxglove

The sinister magical attributes of the foxglove are reflected in some of its many country names, which include 'bloody finger', 'witch's finger', 'fairy cap', 'dead man's bells' and 'little folk's glove'.

Handsome in appearance but poisonous if misused, the dual nature of the flower is neatly expressed in the language of flowers, in which it signifies insincerity.

The distinctive shape of the flowers have inspired all sorts of poetic fancies. For the seventeenth-century British poet Abraham Cowley it was essential wearing for Flora, the Roman goddess of flowers and spring:

'The Foxglove on fair Flora's hand is worn,
Lest while she gathers flowers she meets a thorn.'

A popular belief, expressed in its country name – 'little folk's glove' – was that its flowers were donned by the faeries. According to the nineteenth-century British poet Hartley Coleridge, however, they preferred to 'sweetly nestle in Foxglove bells'.

The toxic properties of the foxglove have long linked it with witches, who traditionally used it in magic potions to hallucinogenic effect. Their 'flying ointment' was composed of foxglove and other 'baneful' herbs. To ensure the plant's potency, they were always careful to pick it with the left hand from the north side of a hedge.

Ruled by Venus, the foxglove was believed to have a regulatory effect on the heart. Its leaves can safely be used in poultices to calm headaches. Digitalin, the drug made from the flower, is now an important heart stimulant, widely used in modern medicine.

Poppy

Legend has it that the brilliant red corn poppy was born from the blood of a dragon. In mythology, the opium poppy was the plant of sleep and dreams. The horned poppy, according to the seventeenth-century British dramatist Ben Jonson in 'Witches' Song', was a favourite ingredient in black magic:

'Yes, I have brought to help our vows,
Horned poppy, Cypress bough,
The fig tree wild that grows on tombs,
And juice which from the larch tree comes.'

A milky juice can be obtained from the common red poppy that possesses narcotic properties but to a much lesser degree than the opium poppy, which has been used as a powerful narcotic for centuries. The leaves and petals of the common poppy in herbal medicine can be drunk as an infusion to treat respiratory complaints.

Ruled by the moon, the poppy is believed to possess magical powers of prophecy. One charm is to cut a hole in a dried pod, remove the poppy seeds and put a small piece of yellow paper containing the question to be answered inside it. Lay the prepared pod beside the bed and the answer will be revealed in a dream during the night.

Poppy leaves were crushed in the hand in love divination charms, as the ancient Greek poet Theocritus noted:

'By a prophetic poppy leaf I found
Your changed affection, for it gave no sound.
Though in my hand struck hollow as it lay,
But quickly withered like your love away.'

Rosemary

'There's rosemary, that's for remembrance;
Pray love, remember.'
HAMLET, WILLIAM SHAKESPEARE

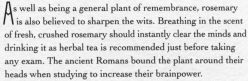

As well as being a general plant of remembrance, rosemary is also believed to sharpen the wits. Breathing in the scent of fresh, crushed rosemary should instantly clear the minds and drinking it as herbal tea is recommended just before taking any exam. The ancient Romans bound the plant around their heads when studying to increase their brainpower.

Ruled by the sun, the herb was traditionally used as a love oracle. A bowl of flour placed under a rosemary bush on Midsummer Eve should reveal the initials of a future spouse, when checked the next day.

A more elaborate love spell, to be cast on St Agnes Eve, promises the dream vision of a future husband or wife. A sprig of rosemary and a sixpence must be placed under the pillow. Another sprig of rosemary is placed in one shoe, and a sprig of thyme is placed in the other shoe, both are sprinkled with water and the shoes are set on opposite sides of the bed, while chanting:

'St Agnes, that's to lovers kind,
Come ease the troubles of my mind.'

The seventeenth-century English herbalist Nicholas Culpeper had such faith in the medicinal powers of rosemary that he recommended making a conserve of the leaves and flowers to avoid catching bubonic plague. As a result, when the plague swept through London, the price of a bunch of rosemary soared, making it too expensive for most people to buy.

Rosemary is a symbol of the Nativity of Christ. The Virgin Mary was believed to have hidden with the infant Jesus under a bush when pursued by Herod's soldiers. In early Christian churches, sprigs formed an important part of floral garlands to ward off witches. The herb was popularly used to crown the wassail bowl, or toasting cup, used for festivities.

married love. She concealed dead children in strawberry leaves and smuggled them in the clouds to heaven.

Strawberries are specifically linked to the elves in Bavaria, where a farmer customarily tied a basket of the fruit between the cow's horns when it grazed on upland pastures, as a gift for the elves. In return, they would ensure it yielded an abundant supply of milk.

Yarrow

A favourite faery flower, yarrow has long been a staple of love charms, and is said to have the power to keep a couple happily together for seven years if eaten at the wedding.

The plant stem was traditionally used as a love oracle. If it was cut crosswise, it was claimed, the initials of a future husband or wife would magically appear. Another charm, which promised to supply the answer by dream, was to place one ounce of yarrow under the pillow and recite:

'Thou pretty herb of Venus-tree,
Thy true name is Yarrow;
Now who my bosom friend must be,
Pray tell thou me tomorrow.'

Ruled by Venus, yarrow was also believed to possess magical powers of protection, and it was woven into floral garlands hung up in homes and churches on Midsummer Eve to ward off evil spirits. If held in the hand it could stop all fear.

Herbalists recommended pushing yarrow up the nose to make it bleed as an antidote to migraine, from which the plant gained its alternative country name 'nosebleed'. This practice was also used as a means of love divination, as described in this country rhyme:

'Green "arrow, green" arrow, you bears a white blow
If my love loves me my nose will bleed now.'

Strawberry

Both the wild and garden varieties of strawberry are much prized by herbalists for their cooling qualities. A tisane of leaves can be drunk to combat fevers and excessive perspiration. The leaves are also believed to have a tonic effect on the blood.

Strawberry juice may improve the complexion. It should be smeared over the face at night and washed off with chervil water in the morning. The juice can also be used to brighten discoloured teeth.

Ruled by Venus, the strawberry symbolises love and perfection. In Christian tradition the plant was the emblem of the good fruits of the Holy Spirit. In Norse mythology it was sacred to Frigg, the goddess of the clouds and of

Lavender

This aromatic plant gained its name from the Latin *lavare*, meaning 'to wash', from the ancient custom of scenting bathwater with its leaves and flowers. Lavender also dries well and lavender bags have long been used to keep linen smelling sweet.

The powerful aroma of burning lavender was reputed to be sufficiently potent to keep witches away and it was used on Midsummer Eve bonfires. Brides were advised to bring lavender into the home for protection against marital cruelty.

But legend warned that, if the plant thrived in a garden the daughter of the house would never marry, inspiring the popular saying: 'Lavender will grow in an old maid's garden'. At one time, it was carried together with rosemary to preserve chastity.

Despite such beliefs, lavender was regarded as a lover's flower by the Elizabethans, as noted in this popular song of the time:

'Lavender is for lovers true,
Which evermore be fain,
Desiring always for to have
Some pleasure for their pain.'

Ruled by Mercury, lavender signifies distrust, acknowledge-ment and assiduity in the language of flowers. Herbalists have been happy to put their faith in its healing powers, however. The plant has long been used as a nerve tonic in combination with rosemary, crushed cinnamon and nutmeg in the form of a tincture. Dabbed on the forehead, it should ease nervous headaches and swiftly calm a fever.

Carnation

'The fairest flowers o'the season
Are our carnations'
THE WINTER'S TALE, WILLIAM SHAKESPEARE

According to Christian tradition, the carnation sprang from the tears shed by Mary on her way to Calvary, since when the pink carnation has become the symbol of mother love.

The carnation has long been used as a plant of magical protection. Red carnations in a garden are said to ward off negative influences. Witches had such faith in the plant's power that they wore it to prevent an untimely death on the scaffold.

Ruled by the sun, the carnation is a potent ingredient in magic spells. It can be anointed as an oil to promote power. Carnation oil was traditionally used to restore energy, to aid healing and was regularly applied in consecration ceremonies.

To ensure the magical potency of a carnation, it should be planted during the first quarter of the new moon and in the sign of Libra to produce the most fragrant flowers.

Honeysuckle

Fragrant honeysuckle – 'luscious woodbine' – garlanded
Titania's faery bed and helped to inspire her dreams of
love. In the language of flowers it signifies the bond of love,
and the gift of a sweet-smelling bouquet meant 'We belong
to each other'.

Its strong perfume was believed by some to ward off
evil spirits. Scottish farmers used to hang up honeysuckle
to protect their cattle from witchcraft. In faery lore,
releasing the scent by lightly crushing the fresh flowers
and rubbing them on the forehead was said to heighten
clairvoyant powers.

Ruled by Jupiter, honeysuckle is also used in spells
of prosperity. A charm to attract money is to light green
candles, ringed by a garland of woodbine; the flowers are
also a favourite ingredient of prosperity sachets.

Appropriately, herbalists prescribe honeysuckle as a
powerful tonic for the heart. It is suggested as a remedy for
most cardiac disorders. The sweet-tasting flowers can be
eaten raw, or taken as a dessert spoonful of syrup daily.
Drinking two cupfuls daily of an infusion of the bark, or
applying a poultice of the leaves, is also believed to reduce
swellings. Avoid honeysuckle berries, however, as some
varieties are poisonous.

Snapdragon

The snapping jaws of snapdragon are held to be a powerful
counter-charm to ward off witches. They will also stay away,
it is said, if the flower is stepped on when evil threatens.

The distinctive flowers inspired a host of country names,
including 'lion's snap', 'bulldogs' and 'toad's mouth'. The
seventeenth-century British poet Abraham Cowley
celebrated some of them in a verse dedicated to the plant:

'Antirrhinum, more modest takes the style
Of Lion's mouth, sometimes of Calf's snout-vile,
By us Snapdragon called, to make amends
But say what this chimera name intends?'

The name 'calf's snout' referred to the shape of the seed pods
rather than the flowers. The pods were also compared by a
contemporary to the 'old bones of a Sheep's head that hath
long been in the water, or the flesh consumed cleane away'.

Ruled by Venus, the snapdragon symbolises
indiscretion, presumption and simply 'no' in
the language of flowers. These qualities were
recognised by the ancient Greek writer
Theophrastus, who noted that 'some men have
supposed that the use of this herb should help
men to obtain praise and worship ... the
dreams of sorcerers'.

Rose

The 'Queen of Flowers', the rose symbolises beauty, youth and love in mythological beliefs around the world.

According to Greek legend, Chloris, the goddess of flowers, created the rose by transforming a beautiful dead nymph into the most gorgeous of flowers and crowning it with a diadem of dewdrops. Delighted by the glorious bloom, Aphrodite, the goddess of love, presented the rose to Eros, the god of love.

The rose has always been most closely identified with love and youthful passion, as the sixteenth-century British poet Edmund Spenser makes clear:

'Gather therefore the Rose, whilst yet is prime,
For soon comes age, that will her pride deflower:
Gather the Rose of love, whilst yet is time,
Whilst loving thou mayest loved be with
equal crime.'

In the language of the flowers, the gift of a rosebud means 'You are young and beautiful', and a full-blown rose stands for beauty and engagement; a rose thorn, however, signifies death and suffering.

Ruled by Venus, the rose empowers spells of love, fertility and clairvoyance. A traditional charm to attract love is to mix rose petals with patchouli, cinnamon and red sandalwood on a Friday during the waxing of the moon, and to burn the mixture as a love incense.

The heady perfume of the rose has long made it a favourite ingredient for potions and perfumes. Attar, the oil of the damask rose, an ointment of rose oil, rose water and honey, was was considered the most precious of all Persian perfumes. In faery lore, burning rose oil over charcoal on a Friday night will infuse your home with loving vibrations.

Meadowsweet

Ruled by Jupiter and commonly known as 'Queen of the Meadows', this fragrant flower is said to possess very gentle magic vibrations, and is traditionally arranged on a magic altar when mixing love charms. However, the strong scent of meadowsweet has also lent it darker associations. The plant has been linked with death, and its perfume was believed to induce a deep and fatal sleep under certain circumstances. For the nineteenth-century British poet Algernon Swinburne, it was a funerary flower:

'Shall I strew on thee rose or rue or laurel,
Brother, on this that was the veil of thee?
Or quiet sea-flower moulded by the sea,
Or simplest growth of meadow-sweet or sorrel?'

Irish tradition suggests that it was the moon goddess Aine of Knockaine, the guardian spirit of crops and cattle, who endowed the flower with its distinctive fragrance.

Meadowsweet has had many uses. In Nottinghamshire the blossom was traditionally dried and smoked like tobacco. In herbal medicine it is a powerful remedy for an upset stomach when taken as an infusion. Meadowseet beer has long been a popular country drink.

Mugwort

Also known as 'witch herb', mugwort is traditionally associated with midsummer magic. If the juice of the young leaves is rubbed on a magic mirror or a crystal ball it is believed to strengthen clairvoyant powers.

Mugwort is a popular ingredient of love charms. One complicated charm was to collect the rare coal that magically appeared under the plant during one hour of the year, then place it under the pillow to inspire a dream of a future spouse. The plant is ruled by Venus, who is sometimes depicted with a spray of mugwort in her hand. Its potent magical powers were conjured in the country rhyme:

'Thou hast might for three and against thirty.
For thy venom availest for plying vile things.'

Marigold

A flower of the sun, the marigold was popularly known as the 'Bride of the Sun', from its habit of opening its petals at sunrise and closing them at sunset.

Ruled by the sun, it signifies prosperity and success in the language of flowers. To dream of marigolds is said to portend a happy marriage. Marigold oil is also used in a magic love spell to inspire a dream to identify a future spouse, but the spell must be carried out on 18 October, the day dedicated to St Luke, the lucky saint for lovers. Before going to bed, the stomach, breast and hips should be anointed with the oil and these words spoken:

'St Luke, St Luke be kind to me,
In dreams let me my true love see.'

In Christianity, the marigold was believed to derive its name from the Virgin Mary, as the eighteenth-century British poet John Gay noted:

'What flower is that which bears the Virgin's name,
The richest metal added to the name?'

The vibrant colour of its petals was thought to give strength and comfort to people suffering from depression, and it is used to build a positive aura in spell-casting. The flowers must be picked at noon to ensure their potency.

In herbal medicine, the petals can be eaten or taken as an infusion, or applied as an oil or lotion. Petals applied as a lotion are said to be good for the complexion. Eating marigold jam is believed to ward off witches.

Autumn

Fly Agaric

The magic mushroom fly agaric has been used in secret rituals all over the world for many years. Revered as a plant of great mystical significance, mainly because of its hallucinogenic properties, the Druids are believed to have employed it as an aid to divination, but were careful to dry the mushroom before consuming it. Eaten fresh, it causes severe vomiting, rapid breathing and delirium.

In Russia, the shaman magicians used fly agaric to empower them. Its potency was celebrated in this legend, in which it was used to help a stranded whale:

'Big Raven caught a whale but he could not send it to its home in the sea. He was unable to lift the grass bag containing travelling provisions for it. Big Raven called to Existence to help. Existence said: "Go to a level place near the sea; there you will find soft white stalks with red and white spotted hats. These are spirits, the Wapag. Eat some and they will help you."'

Ruled by the moon, fly agaric is brewed into a tea, which is drunk by witches before their rituals of admission, and as an aid to clairvoyance.

Apple

The forbidden fruit of the Christian Garden of Eden, the apple also has powerful magical associations. In Greek mythology, the magical Golden Apples of the Hesperides were guarded against all comers by the three Nymphs of the Setting Sun, in an orchard on the Islands of the Blessed. Equally potent in Norse mythology, the sacred apple was eaten daily by the gods and goddesses of Asgard because it contained the gift of eternal youth. The Celts regarded the apple as 'the noblest of trees' because it was the bearer of life-giving fruit. To fell an apple tree was punishable by death.

Strong apple cider is popularly referred to as 'witches' brew'. The apple is revered as a magical fruit, because when cut open it reveals the symbol of the five-pointed star, or pentagram.

Also known as the 'Tree of Love', the apple is ruled by Venus. A popular charm to promote true love is to give your sweetheart an apple, divide it up and for each to eat half of it at the same time. The nineteenth-century British poet Christina Rossetti celebrated its romantic aspect:

*'My heart is like an apple-tree
Whose boughs are bent with thickset fruit.'*

Apple blossom is often added as an empowering ingredient to love and healing charms. The fruit is also used as a magical aid to fertility. Barren women were advised to roll themselves on the ground under a solitary apple tree in order to become pregnant.

Apple cider can be used instead of wine or blood in magical spells, and pouring cider on newly dug ground is thought to make it more fruitful. On the Twelfth Night, after Christmas, cakes are customarily placed in an apple tree and cider is poured on it, as a magical libation to ensure a good crop in the coming year. During the ceremony, pots and pans should be banged loudly to drive evil spirits away.

Heliotrope

The symbol of eternal love, heliotrope was born from the constancy of the water nymph Clytie in Greek myth. Clytie loved the sun god Helios but was abandoned by him. Heartbroken, she fasted for nine days and nine nights until, pitying her grief, the other gods transformed her into a heliotrope, 'the flower which follows the sun'.

Ruled by the sun, the flower is said to follow its course throughout the day, as noted in this traditional rhyme:

'There is a flower, whose modest eye
Is turned with looks of light and love,
Who breathes her softest, sweetest sigh,
Whene'er the sun is bright above.'

Heliotrope is believed to aid clairvoyance. A traditional charm was to put a flower under the pillow to induce prophetic dreams. It was also said that placing heliotrope in a church would magically reveal those who had not been true to their wedding vows.

Blackberry

Folk legend warns that it is unlucky to eat blackberries after Michaelmas Day at the end of September, as that was when the Devil fell into a bramble bush when he was ousted from Heaven. He was badly scratched and spat on the berries in revenge. The belief was celebrated in this Scottish rhyme:

'Oh weans! Oh weans! the morn's the Fair
Ye may na eat the berries mair
This nicht the Deil gangs ower them a'
To tough them with his pooshioned paw.'

Ruled by Venus, the plant signifies envy and jealousy in the language of flowers and it is a gift of bad luck for a woman. More positively, it is believed to possess powers of magical healing. Many of the spells include a spoken charm. To cure whooping cough, it is necessary to crawl through a bramble bush backwards, while reciting:

'In bramble out cough,
Here I leave the whooping cough.'

Nine blackberry leaves dipped in holy water are said to be a cure for burns, if applied one after the other while saying three times to each:

There came three
angels out of the east.
One brought fire and
two brought frost,
Out fire, in frost,
In the name of the Father,
the Son and the Holy Ghost.'

Hop

'The sun in the south or else southlie and west
Is joy to the Hop, as welcomed ghest
But wind in the north, or else northerly east,
To Hop is as ill as a fray in a feast.'
FIVE HUNDRETH GOOD POINTES OF HUSBANDRIE

Young hop shoots were eaten as a delicacy by the Romans, but the plant is now best known as a vital ingredient of beer.

Many superstitions and customs were traditionally associated with the harvesting of hops. Visitors to the fields were required to contribute 'foot money' to keep the field lucky and boost the yield, and the pickers customarily kept a twisted stem as a good-luck charm. Traditionally, the harvest supper held to celebrate the end of picking concluded with a ceremony to promote love and fertility, in which a young couple would be plunged into the hop bins. The country custom inspired the following lines by the eighteenth-century British poet Christopher Smart:

'The exulting band
Of pickers, male and female, seize the fair
Reluctant, and with boist'rous force and brute
By cries unmoved, they bury her i' the bin
Nor does the youth escape – him too they seize
And in such posture place as best may serve
To hide his charmer's blushes.'

Ruled by Mars, the hop is used by herbalists to treat heart disease and hop tea is recommended as a sedative. Hop blossom stuffed inside a pillow is supposed to be a good cure for insomnia.

Hazel nuts are considered to be the source of magical wisdom and fertility. Finn, the legendary Irish leader, was said to have gained his magic tooth by accidentally tasting the salmon of knowledge that fed on hazel nuts.

Hazel is ruled by the sun. Its nuts are used by herbalists to prevent hardening of the arteries. In magic, they are added to purslane, jasmine, periwinkle and anemone to make love potions.

In *Romeo and Juliet*, Shakespeare provided his diminutive faery Queen Mab with a hazel-nut carriage:

'Her chariot is an empty hazel-nut,
Made by the joiner squirrel or old grub,
Time out o' mind the fairies' coach-makers.'

Bryony

The red berries of the climbing bryony brighten the autumn landscape, but the plant is most prized in magic for its root, which has long been used as an easier alternative to mandrake. The exotic mandrake root is supposed to produce such wild shrieks when pulled from the ground that it induces madness. The only way to harvest it in safety is to tie a dog to the plant on a moonless night to pull it up.

Bryony root, also known as 'Devil's Turnip', was used by witches to make a potion to create an 'ugly image' of their intended victim, as described in this traditional verse:

'Witches which some murther do intend
Doe make a picture and doe shoote at it;
And in that part where they the picture hit,
The partie's self doth languish to his end.'

Ruled by Mars, the plant symbolises prosperity. According to one magic charm, if the root is placed upon a coin it will increase riches. It is also reputed to possess strong powers of healing and at one time was employed as a cure for leprosy. The juice from the stem is used to banish warts in herbal medicine, and a pound of fresh root boiled in water can be used as the 'best purge for horned cattle'.

Hazel

The hazel tree is one of the most powerful magic trees and furnishes the best material for magic wands. A rod made from a forked hazel branch was traditionally believed to possess supernatural powers of divination. Such rods have been widely used for many centuries as dousing sticks to identify underground water sources. To ensure its potency, however, the rod must be cut from the tree on St John's Eve.

Hazel wood and hazel nuts are thought to offer protection against witchcraft. Horses traditionally wore hazel breast-bands as counter charms, and cattle were singed with hazel rods fresh from Midsummer Eve fires as a magical safeguard. In Scotland, it was believed that an effective way of getting rid of witches was to throw double hazel nuts at them.

Rowan

The rowan, or mountain ash, was traditionally known as the 'witchentree', and was planted as a protection against evil spirits. Its wood is also said to make the most powerful witch's wand.

The name rowan derives from the old Norse word *runa*, which means a charm. Its berries were considered to be one of the sacred foods of the gods in classical myth, and the Druids believed the tree possessed great magical and divinatory powers.

Ruled by the sun, the rowan was often planted close to the house as a magical safeguard. Protective branches were also hung above the front door, and also in cattle sheds to protect the animals. Cows are thought to be most at risk at Beltane, the eve of Mayday, when witches like to steal their milk for use in their magic rites. In addition to hanging protective branches of rowan over the cattle, the animals can be further protected by tying two twigs of rowan together with red thread to form an equal-armed cross, and attaching it to the tail.

A bewitched animal can only be controlled by a rowan wand. To ensure the wood's potency, however, it must always be broken away from the tree by hand rather than cut, and it is vital to ask for permission first. An equal-armed cross of rowan twigs tied together with red thread also offers a good charm of personal protection. It is empowered by reciting:

'Rowan tree and scarlet thread,
I conjure thee to be a protection
And safeguard against adversity and evil.
Protect me well.'

All parts of the tree can be used to magical effect. Crushed and dried pine needles mixed with equal parts of juniper and cedar are burnt together in the hearth from 1 November to 21 March to purify the home. The crushed needles can also be added to a bag of seasonal herbs for a magical winter bath of cleansing.

Pine cones can be carried as fertility charms and the nuts can also be eaten to promote pregnancy. Branches of pine are traditionally used to sweep the forest floor before performing magical rites outdoors.

Fern

The magical strength of the fern, which is ruled by Saturn, is believed to be strongest during the summer and winter solstices, when the plant is imbued with the potency of gold and fire. At Christmas it symbolises the hidden fire of the winter sun. In summer, if gathered within three days of Midsummer Eve, the fern should glow like a golden fire. Whoever holds such a plant on Midsummer Eve and then climbs a mountain, will discover a vein of gold, or see the treasures of the earth bathed in blue flames.

The plant's magical potency arose largely from the miraculous way in which it reproduces itself by apparently invisible seeds, or spores. This inspired the belief that anyone who swallowed a fern seed would become invisible, as Shakespeare noted in *Henry IV Part 1*:

'We have the receipt of fern-seed,
We walk invisible.'

The maidenhair fern was one of the magic plants of Roman myth. It was believed to be the hair of Venus, goddess of love and beauty, and it is still called 'cheveux de Venus' in French. The belief is based on the extraordinary effect water has on the plant. When placed underwater, its foliage takes on a magic silvery sheen, but when removed it is perfectly dry. A Roman magic potion for grace, beauty and love was empowered by adding powdered maidenhair fern.

Pine

Ruled by Mars, the pine signifies boldness and fidelity in the language of flowers. Both qualities were celebrated in these lines by the nineteenth-century American poet Bret Harte:

'And on that grave where English oak and holly
And laurel wreaths entwine
Deem it not all a too presumptuous folly,
This spray of western pine.'

Holly

'Heigh-ho! sing, heigh-ho! unto the green holly:
Most friendship is feigning, most loving mere folly.
Then heigh-ho! the holly!
This life is most jolly.'
AS YOU LIKE IT, WILLIAM SHAKESPEARE

The bleak tone of this song is at odds with the popular notion of the holly as a symbol of joy. But it echoes the more worrying aspect of the plant suggested by its two meanings in the language of flowers, which are foresight and 'I dare not approach'.

The evergreen berried holly is now most closely associated with festive Christmas celebrations. As a potent symbol of life in winter, however, it traditionally played a major role in the pagan celebrations of the winter solstice, 'the door of the gods', which symbolised ascent and the growing power of the sun.

Ruled by Mars, holly has long been regarded as providing magical protection against evil. The tree was commonly planted close to the house as a counter charm and it was considered unlucky to fell it. Berried sprigs can be hung indoors to celebrate Christmas but they should never be brought into the home before Christmas Eve and must always be removed before Twelfth Night. The rule does not apply to churches, however, where it is possible to leave holly sprigs *in situ* until just before Candlemas at the beginning of February without courting disaster.

The Roman writer Pliny identified the holly early on as a plant of protection against both witches and lightning. Its leaves and berries have also long been used as magical aids to heighten masculinity. The berries are used by modern herbalists to suppress fevers. The dried leaves mixed with tea are employed as a restorative tonic.

Ivy

Greek myth claims that the ivy is named after a nymph who danced with such joy for Dionysus, god of wine, that she fell dead from exhaustion at his feet. Moved by her sacrifice, Dionysus transformed her into the ivy, a plant that joyfully embraces everything around it. Ivy can have an intoxicating effect when eaten, and it played a role in the orgiastic rites of Bacchus and Dionysus.

Ruled by Saturn, ivy signifies attachment and eternal friendship, and means 'I die where I cling' in the language of flowers. An ivy leaf can be used as a love oracle. A young woman who puts one in her pocket and goes out for a walk should fall in love with the first man she meets.

Ivy grown on the walls of a house provides magical protection for those within, but if it dies bad luck will swiftly follow. It is also used as a potent divination plant. A seventeenth-century spell recommends putting a leaf in a dish of water on New Year's Eve and then checking it on Twelfth Night:

'If the said Leafe be fair and green as it was before, for then you, or the party for whome you lay it into the Water, will be whole and sound, and safe from any sicknesse all the next yeare.'

Herbalists warn that only a small quantity of ivy should ever be used due to its potentially toxic effects. A safe combination of five leaves infused in half a pint of water calm fevers.

Mistletoe

The Druids believed mistletoe to be a magic plant, and ceremonially cut it six days after the new moon with a golden sickle for their sacrificial rites, as noted in this popular rhyme:

'The fearless British priests, under the aged oak,
Taking a milk-white bull, unstained with the yoke,
And with an axe of gold, from that Jove-sacred tree
The Mistletoe cut down.'

Ruled by the sun, mistletoe is traditionally linked with fertility and protection. The Druids believed that its berries were the fertilising dew of the supreme deity, and their potency inspired the Christmas custom of lovers kissing under a berried branch to make their romance blossom. For the magic to work, however, they must remove a berry after each kiss and throw it over the left shoulder. Women were advised to wear necklaces and bracelets of mistletoe to help them conceive.

The Druids distributed the mistletoe used in their rites to their followers to hang up as protection in their homes. The plant can also be worn around the neck as a potent counter charm, but before cutting the plant the wearer must walk three times around the host tree and be sure to cut what is needed with a new dagger.

Mistletoe was chief of the seven sacred herbs of the Druids, the others being vervain, henbane, primrose, pulsatilla, clover and wolfsbane. Herbalists use an infusion of diced leaves and young branches as a heart tonic and to reduce high blood pressure. The juice of the berries can be dabbed on the skin to remove obstinate pimples; if massaged in, it is said to ease stiff joints.

Snowdrop

In Christian tradition the snowdrop is dedicated to the Virgin Mary. At the Feast of Purification on Candlemas Day, her image was ceremonially taken down and snowdrops were strewn in its place. A bowl of snowdrops brought into the house at Candlemas was believed to confer 'white purification' on the house.

Ruled by Saturn, the snowdrop symbolises friendship in adversity and purity in the language of flowers, as the nineteenth-century British poet Lord Tennyson made clear:

'Make thou my spirit pure and clean,
As are the frosty skies,
Or the first snowdrop of the year
That in my bosom lies.'

The shape of the flower was thought by some to resemble a shroud, and it was believed to be unlucky to bring only one snowdrop into the house for that reason. Girls who wished to marry in the same year were also warned not to pick a snowdrop before St Valentine's Day, as it would blight their romantic prospects.

Appropriately, the snowdrop is used in herbal medicine to combat discomforts caused by cold weather. An ointment prepared from the crushed bulbs is said to cure frostbite and chilblains.

Aconite

The winter aconite was originally identified with the poisonous herb dedicated to Hecate, the patron goddess of magic and witchcraft. This more sinister form, also known as monkshood, is said to grow where the saliva fell from Cerberus, the monstrous guard dog of the Underworld.

Reflecting its original botanical classification, the golden aconite was more commonly known as winter wolfsbane, and the flowers were described by the sixteenth-century herbalist Henry Lyte as 'these venomous and naughtie herbs'.

In the language of flowers, the plant signifies lustre, and the sight of its bright yellow flowers blooming in the dead of winter has cheered many writers, including the nineteenth-century poet John Clare:

'Buttercup flowers that shut at night
And green leaf frilling round their cups of gold.'

Crocus

According to Greek legend, the flower was named by the gods to commemorate Crocus, a handsome youth who died of heartbreak due to his unrequited love for a local shepherdess. The myth inspired both the ancient custom of using crocus flowers to decorate the marriage bed, and also the popular belief that it was a potent love plant. The ancient Romans employed the flower both as a tonic for the heart and a potent love potion.

Ruled by the sun, the crocus signifies youthful attachment and gladness in the language of flowers. The saffron crocus was employed by eleventh-century court ladies as a hair dye, but it has much more powerful magical uses. The plant can be used to raise winds by throwing it high into the air from a lofty place, or by burning it and watching the smoke rise upwards.

Saffron crocus can be ground together with myrrh and rose buds to burn as a healing magic incense. Or it can be drunk as a tea to induce clairvoyance. Before conducting a magic healing rite, it is advisable to wash the hands in purifying saffron water.

Part Three

PLANT A FAERY GARDEN

Follow the magic guidelines to plan your own faery garden.
But be careful to abide by the rules; prepare the land with due reverence
and let the movements of the heavens influence the rhythm of
your planting and harvesting.
These three gardens, if cultivated wisely, will reward you in every way.
Gather the plants to create charms and potions that promise
to change the course of your life. Use the enchanted space the plants
provide as your magic altar. Drink in their potent perfume
and be wafted to a higher plane.

Faery Garden Planting Tips

The ancient belief that the ways of men and plants are influenced by the stars must be respected when planting for magic. To ensure the potency of their herbs, magicial practitioners have always picked the necessary leaves and flowers at sunrise – the magical time when day and night divide and the early-morning dew has just dried.

Both plants and men were traditionally thought to be moon-governed, and the right astrological timing was said to be crucial in ensuring a plentiful crop. The sixteenth-century British farmer Thomas Tusser laid down specific rules for planetary-guided planting in his garden book *Five Hundred Points of Good Husbandrie*:

'Sow peason and beanes in the wane of the moone,
Who soweth them sooner, he soweth too soone,
That they with the planet may rest and arise,
And flourish with bearing most plentiful wise.'

Similar planting guidelines were upheld in the seventeenth century by the British antiquary John Aubrey, who noted that 'if a plant be not gathered according to the rules of astrology, it hath little or no virtue in it'. His contemporary, the famous herbalist Nicholas Culpeper, also insisted that 'he that would know the reason of the Operation of the Herbs, must look up as high as the Stars, astrologically'.

The moon association persists to this day, and extensive trials support some of the old customs. It has been found that, given the same moisture conditions, it is better to sow or plant during a waxing moon, preferably two days before the full moon, except after September, when it is best to sow or plant two days before the new moon.

Most modern farmers may no longer be guided by the stars, but astrological botany still influences magic rites. True adepts take care to learn which planet rules each plant in order to identify how it can be used most potently. The best times to plant are when the moon is in the moist and fertile signs of the zodiac: Cancer, Scorpio, Pisces, Taurus and Capricorn. The most dedicated will also check that the planetary conditions are at their most auspicious before setting out to harvest, in order to avoid any adverse astrological positioning that might deplete the plant's powers.

Planting a Magic Garden

Special preparations are required when planning and planting your plot. Ideally, it should be circular. The circle is central to magical belief, according to the ancient Egyptian wizard Hermes Trismegistus: 'God is a circle whose centre is everywhere and circumference is nowhere.'

The leading twentieth-century American authority on herbal magic Scott Cunningham recommends the following:

Firstly, encircle the plot with a long rope and knot the ends firmly to bind the power within it. Then, sprinkle ground-up mistletoe over the area before digging it. When you have finished digging and your plot is ready for planting, mark each of the four compass points north, south, east and west on its circumference with a stone. Wait until nightfall, then plant a candle outside the circle at the north stone and light it. Do the same at the other three stones, moving clockwise.

Stand in the centre of the circle, facing north. Holding your magic knife, raise your arms skyward and say: "I call upon the powers of the north to bless and protect this garden." Repeat for the east, south and west.

Then, using the point of your knife, trace this pentagram (see illustration), making sure that the uppermost point touches the north candle and that the other points, evenly spaced, touch the rope. Kneel in the southern section of the pentagram to trace the five symbols within it, making sure the top symbol touches the crossing line, as shown.

Sit quietly for ninety heartbeats. Then blow out the candles, starting at the north and moving clockwise. Using a new broom and moving clockwise brush away the pentagram and symbols, and gather up the rope and candles.

Return to your plot next morning at sunrise. Search the ground for fresh magical symbols that may have appeared overnight and record them. They are the links between your garden and the silent forces of nature.

Pour one quart of unfiltered fermented apple cider into an earthenware pot and stand in the middle of your garden. Turning on the central point, sprinkle the cider, which represents revitalising new blood, over the ground with your stong hand.

Leave the garden untouched for three days, making sure that no person or animals walks on it. On the fourth day, begin planting.'

The Faery Potions Garden

Plants grow all around us, but few of us realise how valuable they can be. The inner magic of plants has been well documented over the centuries, and that vast body of accumulated wisdom continues to be a potent source of inspiration. Wield that magical knowledge to cultivate your very own faery potions plot and knot its energy within by planting four intertwined beds, each dedicated to a different aspect of plant magic. Site a moon dial at its epicentre and pave it with glittering sand and crushed sea shells to invoke the potency of the all-powerful ocean and to add a shimmering lustre to your nocturnal rites. Fill your first plot with plants of love, fill your second plot with plants of magical protection, fill your third plot with plants of healing, and fill your fourth plot with plants to soothe the soul.

Plants for the Love Spells Plot

Orpine (Sedum)

Rose (Rosa gallica var. officinalis)

Pansy (Viola tricolor)

Parsley (Petroselinum crispum)

Sage (Salvia officinalis)

Rosemary (Rosmarinus officinalis)

Thyme (Thymus vulgaris)

Commonly known as the Apothecary's Rose, this variety is one of the oldest in cultivation and dates back to the thirteenth century. Its rich fragrance has made it a favourite ingredient in rose-scented oils and potions. The petals still perfume some of the most popular pot-pourri mixes.

Only pluck the most perfect flowerhead when making magic and be sure to pick it at the most auspicious time. This can be spelled out in precise detail, as the opening of this nineteenth-century love divination charm makes clear:

'Gather your rose on the 27th of June, let it be full blown, and as bright red as you can get; pluck it between the hours of three and four in the morning, taking care to have no witness to the transaction.'

Magic numbers empower a more recent spell conjured by strewing five red roses along the path to your loved one's home, while calling his or her name. Five petals from a sixth rose should then be burnt in the flame of a beeswax candle, while chanting:

'Burn a pathway to my door, five petals now are four.
Four to three in candle fire, bringing closer
my desire. Three to two, I burn the rose,
love no hesitation shows. Burn two to one,
till there are none, the spell is done.
Come lover, come.'

Dreams of love can be conjured in many ways, but culti-vating plants traditionally associated with romance must be one of the most pleasurable.

Scent can be a powerful aphrodisiac, and the fragrant rose has come to symbolise love itself. The rose takes centre stage in this small but potent plot, which features seven different flowers and herbs traditionally linked with love. Seven is the most mystical and magical number in spellcasting, but odd numbers are also auspicious and the plants listed can can be grown in groups to provide a more abundant display.

Red symbolises passion and vitality, and pink is for love and affection. Plant a pinkish-red variety of *Sedum* to boost its magical properties as a traditional love charm. Country lasses called sedums 'Midsummer Men' and believed that the movement of the fleshy leaves, bending to right or left, indicated the constancy of their lovers.

Music is the food of love and this plot features four popular divination plants listed in a favourite love ballad inspired by an old folk song:

'Where are you going? To Scarborough Fair.
Parsley, sage, rosemary and thyme,
Remember me to a bonny lass there,
For once she was a true love of mine.'

A Victorian love spell empowered by rosemary is to bind a sprig into a colourful nosegay that includes 'some yarrow off a grave', with some of your own hair. Sprinkle the bunch with a few drops of rosemary oil and wear it under your nightcap. Put on clean sheets and linen, and dream a dream that will identify your true love.

Plant the wild pansy and you will possess the potent faery love flower immortalised by Shakespeare in *A Midsummer Night's Dream*:

'Before milk-white, now purple with love's wound,
And maidens call it love-in-idleness.
The juice of it on sleeping eyelids laid
Will make or man or woman madly dote
Upon the next live creature that it sees.'

The Magic Knife

Always use a special knife when cutting plants for making spells, Scott Cunningham recommends:

'The knife should be new and clean with a wooden handle and a steel blade. Immediately after purchase, the knife should be wrapped in a clean white cotton or linen cloth and lie undisturbed until the next Full Moon.

Just after sunset, take the knife to a quiet spot deep in the countryside. Bury it up to the hilt in the earth. Kneel before it, place both hands on the ground on either side and chant:

"I conjure thee, O knife of steel,
By the powers of the earth,
That thou shalt be of service to me
In the magic art of herbalism."

The same incantation is repeated three times. Firstly, when standing facing east at the top of the highest ground, holding the knife aloft. Secondly, when thrusting the blade into a small fire you have made of gathered wood. Thirdly, when dipping the blade into running water and facing west.

The knife is then rewrapped and kept hidden until needed. Keep it sharp and shiny.

Plants for the Magic Protection Plot

Bay (*Laurus nobilis*)

Angelica (*Angelica archangelica*)

Mugwort (*Artemisia vulgaris*)

Garlic (*Allium sativum*)

Ferns (*Polystichum spp*)

Clover (*Trifolium spp*)

St John's Wort (*Hypericum perforatum*)

Snapdragon (*Antirrhinum majus*)

Yarrow (*Achillea millefolium*)

charm strong enough to dissolve the aura of enchantment that the faeries conjure both to disguise reality and to bind their victims to their will.

St John's Wort is another beneficial magic herb, protecting not only against the faeries but also the Devil, as the nineteenth-century British author Sir Walter Scott noted in these lines spoken by a lusty demon lover kept at bay by its potency:

'If you would be true love mine,
Throw away John's Wort and Verbein.'

A popular magic practice charm is to pass St John's Wort through the smoke of a Midsummer Eve fire and then hang it up in the house to ward off evil spirits.

The handsome evergreen bay's protective properties were described by the seventeenth-century English herbalist Nicholas Culpeper, who wrote that 'It resisteth witchcraft very potently, as also all the evils old Saturn can do the body of man, and they are not a few … neither witch nor devil, thunder nor lightning, will hurt a man where a bay tree is'.

Bay leaves can be worn as a magical safeguard, or they can be burnt and scattered on the floor to exorcise evil spirits. Ideally, they should be picked while facing east as the sun rises.

Country people wove the stems of angelica into necklaces to protect their children from bad faeries. Its root can also be worn as a magical safeguard. The plant is said to combat not only the plague but also mad dogs.

Through the centuries, an arsenal of powerful counter charms have been devised to ward off evil spirits. Solitary travellers venturing into faery-haunted places traditionally carried some form of magical protection to ensure they reached their destination safely, and certain plants – including the nine listed here – have long been used as powerful deterrents.

Smallest but most potent is clover. Carrying a three-leaf clover is considered an effective safeguard, but the ultimate protection is provided by the four-leaf clover. This is a

Making a Protection Charm

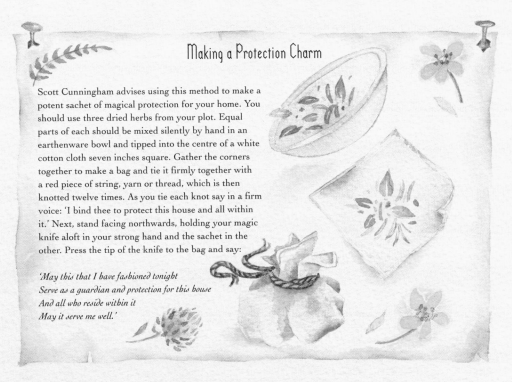

Scott Cunningham advises using this method to make a potent sachet of magical protection for your home. You should use three dried herbs from your plot. Equal parts of each should be mixed silently by hand in an earthenware bowl and tipped into the centre of a white cotton cloth seven inches square. Gather the corners together to make a bag and tie it firmly together with a red piece of string, yarn or thread, which is then knotted twelve times. As you tie each knot say in a firm voice: 'I bind thee to protect this house and all within it.' Next, stand facing northwards, holding your magic knife aloft in your strong hand and the sachet in the other. Press the tip of the knife to the bag and say:

'May this that I have fashioned tonight
Serve as a guardian and protection for this house
And all who reside within it
May it serve me well.'

Mugwort has always been associated with midsummer magic. A plant of safe passage, it was popular with travellers. The Roman writer Pliny noted that 'the wayfaring man that hath the herb tied about him feeleth no weariness at all and he can never be hurt by any poisonous medicine, by any wild beast, neither yet by the sun itself'. The most efficacious sprigs are those picked just before sunrise, during the waxing moon, from a plant leaning northwards.

The folklorist Reginald Scot noted the magical properties of garlic in 1584, writing that many people hung a bulb of garlic 'in the roof of the House, to keep away Witches and Spirits'. Garlic flowers are also used to protect magic altars.

According to medieval textbooks, anyone swallowing a fern seed would be rendered invisible. Ferns can be thrown on hot coals to create an aura of protection, or they can be dried over a midsummer fire and worn as a safeguard.

'The snapdragon, which is much cultivated in gardens on account of its showy flowers, is, in many places, said to have a supernatural influence, and to possess the power of destroying charms,' wrote the Elizabethan folklorist Edward Dyer.

Yarrow was traditionally woven into the floral garlands that decorated homes and churches on Midsummer Eve to guard against evil spirits. Its protective flowers were also strewn across thresholds and fastened to cradles.

Plants for the Healing Plot

Lavender (*Lavandula augustifolia*)

Carnation (*Dianthus caryophyllus*)

Lungwort (*Pulmonaria officinalis*)

Comfrey (*Symphitum offinale*)

Feverfew (*Tanacetum parthenium*)

Woodruff (*Galium odoratum*)

Nasturtium (*Tropaeolum majus*)

The spotted leaves of *Pulmonaria* were thought to resemble lungs, and infusions of its leaves and flowers have traditionally been used to help lung problems.

Lungwort and comfrey are also regarded as magical aids to speed healing. The leaves of either plant can be applied to minor wounds and should reduce scarring.

Eat three to five feverfew leaves in a healing sandwich as a remedy for migraine. To banish headache-inducing stuffiness, carry fragrant spring-flowering woodruff.

Plant red nasturtiums to preserve the magical potency of your healing plot, or eat the edible flowers, as faery garden herbalists have advised, to 'purge the brain and quicken the spirit'.

Gathering Magic Herbs

Scott Cunningham advises the following procedure for collecting your magic herbs:

'Mark the plants you wish to pick and gather them after sunset during the period of the waxing moon to ensure they are fully energised. Fast for three hours beforehand and dress in a white linen robe, or spotlessly clean cotton. Remove your watch

The healing power of plants is well known. Legend has it that their curative powers can be boosted by magic, and these seven plants have figured prominently in spellbooks.

Drink dried lavender, also known as 'elf leaf', as a soothing herbal tea to combat anxiety or depression, or mix it in equal parts with mandrake, peppermint, mugwort, clove, marjoram and orange peel to make a healing sachet to wear around your neck to prevent a headache. Boost your energy levels with the help of sweet-smelling carnations. Anoint youself with carnation oil to empower your healing spells, or pour it on to the dried petals of nine red carnations, smoulder the mixture on a charcoal fire and breathe in the invigorating scent.

The flowers of many plants are reputed to possess positive healing properties in themselves, which can be distilled to produce potions to treat emotional problems. The best-known flower remedies were created by Dr Bach, an eminent British physician, in the 1920s. He wanted his remedies to be a self-help therapy, and he taught his patients how to identify and prepare their own floral potions. The method of making Bach-style flower remedies is very simple. Each of the five plants listed has a different specialist use, but they are all prepared in a similar way.

Gather the flowers of the appropriate variety on a sunny day, ideally when the dew is still on the petals. Avoid touching the plants and cut the flower heads straight into a small clean glass bowl containing thirty millilitres of still mineral water. Add enough to cover the surface and to remain in contact with the water. Stand the bowl beside the trimmed plants and make sure it receives three continuous hours of full

Plants for the Flower Remedy Plot

Heather (Calluna vulgaris)

Impatiens (Impatiens glandulifera)

Rock rose (Helianthemum nummularium)

Hardy plumbago (Ceratostigma willmottianum)

Vervain (Verbena officinalis)

and approach the plant bare-footed. Draw a circle clockwise in the earth around the plant with your magic knife, then recite these words, while touching the blade to the plant: "Thou has grown by favour of the Sun, the Moon, and of the dew. I make this intercession, ye herb: I beseech thee to be of benefit to me and my art, for thy virtues are unfailing. Thou art the dew of all the gods, the eye of the Sun, the light of the Moon, the beauty and glory of the sky, the mystery of the earth. I purify thee so that whatsoever is wrought by me with thee may, in all its powers, have a good and speedy effect with good success. Be purified by my prayer and be powerful." As you cut, state the specific magical use for which the plant is required. Bury a small piece of homemade bread near the base as payment to the Earth.'

sunshine in order to potentise the water. Carefully remove the flowers, using a twig from the plant if possible. Half fill a clean thirty-millilitre bottle with the potentised water and top it up with forty per cent proof brandy to make a mother tincture. Use two drops of the appropriate mother tincture to thirty millilitres of twenty-five per cent proof brandy to make the specific flower remedy. Add two drops of the remedy to any sized glass of water and sip it at intervals.

Use heather to combat fear of loneliness; hardy plumbago to boost self-confidence; impatiens for restless irritability; rock rose to avert panic attacks; and vervain to calm fanaticism.

Queen Titania's Flowery Bower

'I know a bank where the wild thyme blows,
Where oxlips and the nodding violet grows;
Quite over-canopied with luscious woodbine,
With sweet musk-roses and with eglantine:
There sleeps Titania sometime of the night,
Lull'd in these flowers with dances and delight;
An there the snake throws her enamell'd skin,
Weed wide enough to wrap a fairy in.'

A MIDSUMMER NIGHT'S DREAM, WILLIAM SHAKESPEARE

Guided by Oberon's evocative description of his faery queen's
flowery bower in 'A Midsummer Night's Dream', you can plant
your own enchanted bed of sweet-smelling flowers. If Titania's
habit of reclining directly on a bed of flowers strikes you as a little
too magical, why not wrap yourself in a shimmering snakeskin-style
hammock instead. Hang it between two decorative trees that
provide sufficient support for climbing woodbine and musk roses
to scramble up the trunks and entwine together overhead,
creating a floral arch. Plant an aromatic carpet of thyme and dot
it with bushes of fragrant eglantine. Drink in all the different
scents as you rock yourself gently to sleep.

Plants for Queen Titania's Flowery Bower

Wild thyme (*Thymus praecox*)

Eglantine (*Rosa rubigonosa*)

Woodbine (*Lonicera periclymenum*)

Musk rose (*Rosa moschata*)

Wild thyme is full of magic. Anyone wanting to see faeries was traditionally advised to carry a sprig about with them. A highly appropriate herb for a magical bed, it is also said that if you lie down on a faery hill with your eyes closed and put wild thyme on your eyelids, faeries will appear before you.

Thyme dries very well and is a popular addition to pot-pourris. It also makes one of the most beneficial of all tisanes, as it stimulates the circulation and can even speed recovery from a hangover.

Eglantine is the sweet-briar rose with leaves that smell of apples, especially after rain. This variety of rose is an emblem of sweetness in the language of flowers and the gift of eglantine means 'the fragrance of this flower brings memories of you'.

Woodbine is another name for honeysuckle, a plant whose flowers are most powerfully scented at night. In the language of flowers it symbolises love, and the gift of honeysuckle means 'with this I plight my troth'. In folklore the plant is associated with powers of clairvoyance. To induce the state, fresh flowers were lightly crushed and

Midsummer Magic

Midsummer Eve, as Shakspeare well knew, is the most magical time of the year. It is when the days are longest and the nights are shortest, and it was the day that country folk traditionally gathered to celebrate the life-giving power of the sun.

Midsummer was originally celebrated at the summer solstice on 21 June, the day when the sun climbs to its highest point in the sky. With the coming of Christianity, however, the ancient agricultural festival was moved to 24 June, when the feast of St John the Baptist was held, also known as St John's Eve.

The summer solstice still plays a key role in magic ritual. The most popular gathering in Britain is held at Stonehenge, where modern Druids meet on the night before Midsummer to watch the sun rise exactly over the ancient Heel Stone.

Magic bonfires are traditionally lit on Midsummer Eve, when evil spirits are also believed to roam abroad. The herb St John's Wort gained its name from its powers of magical protection on that night. The plant can be passed through the smoke of a Midsummer fire to increase its potency, then hung up to guard the home.

rubbed on the forehead. Honeysuckle arranged inside a house traditionally foretells a wedding, and its scent inspires dreams of love. The fourteenth-century English poet Geoffrey Chaucer described the country custom of girls in search of true love wearing honeysuckle wreaths:

'Wore chaplets on hir hede
Of fresh wodebind, be such never were
To love untrue, he thought, he ded.'

The heady scent of musk rose has made it a favourite ingredient of many magical love potions. A popular concoction is love oil, in which a handful of rose buds are placed in a silver goblet, to which one dram of rose oil is added. The mixture is then left to stand for at least a week. It should be used on a Friday night and burnt on hot charcoal to infuse your home with loving vibrations.

A more luxuriant version of Queen Titania's bed can be planted to equally magical effect, taking advantage of the heady scents released by modern garden varieties. The following plan is just one of many possible plantings.

Plants for an Alternative Flowery Bower

Thyme (*Thymus spp*)

Dwarf rugosa rose (*Rosa 'Max Graf'*)

Night scented stock (*Matthiola bicornis*)

Tobacco plant (*Nicotiana sylvestris*)

Regal lily (*Lilium regale*)

Butterfly bush (*Buddleia fallowiana var alba*)

Japanese honeysuckle (*Lonicera japonioca 'Halliana'*)

Climbing rose (*Rosa 'Constance Spry'*)

Climbing rose (*Rosa 'Guinee'*)

Plant different varieties of thyme to create a multi-coloured aromatic path leading to your faery bed and edge it with fragrant ground-cover roses. Around your bed plant nectar-rich butterfly bushes, interspersed with night-scented stock, tobacco plants and regal lilies. For added comfort, recline on an elegant upholstered 'day bed' and grow honeysuckle and roses up the supporting frame. Then swing yourself gently to sleep as you breathe in all the natural perfumes.

Colour plays a vital role in magical ritual. This planting is predominantly pink, white and yellow, with a dash of deep red. Pink signifies love and affection, white is for blessings, yellow is for mental powers and red is for passion.

The dreams that come to you in your fragrant garden retreat may well feature plants. If so, you can can decipher what they might portend by consulting one of the many magical books concerning the interpretation of dreams. To dream of roses in full bloom signifies a happy marriage, but a withered rose spells bad luck and disappointment. Similarly, if fresh lilies appear to you, wedding bells will not be far off, but if in your dream lilies are past their best, it signifies the death or severe illness of a loved one. If you would prefer not to dream, you can follow this magical procedure recommended in a traditional charm:

'Take vervain and hang it about a man's neck, and let him drink some of the juice before going to bed; certainly he will not dream if he does so.'

Magical Scents

'I cannot see what flowers are at my feet,
Nor what soft incense hangs upon the boughs.'
ODE TO PSYCHE, JOHN KEATS

Queen Titania drifted off to sleep lulled by the perfume of a choice selection of sweetly scented wild flowers. Her faery bed was furnished with fragrant plants that traditionally bloomed in country hedgerows and grassy banks.

Each plant, however, was carefully selected for its distinctive perfume, for scent is a vital component of the faery garden. A powerful stimulus to the senses, the natural fragrance released by flowers has played an important role in magic ritual from time immemorial. Magical oils can be made to retain the full scent and therefore potency of the individual plant and to stimulate different centres of the brain.

Most essential oils are made professionally by distillation, but it is possible to make a milder version at home. Fill a clean glass jar with the leaves and petals of the chosen plant, cover with a carrier oil, such as sweet almond or grapeseed. Cap and leave in a warm place out of sunlight for a week, then strain the oil through muslin into a clean jar and discard the original plant material. If the oil is not scented enough, repeat the same procedure until satisfied, then store the concentrated oil in a cool dark place, ideally in an amber glass jar, ready for use.

To instill your oil with magical potency, Scott Cunningham recommends that you dip the blade of a magic knife into the oil, then raise it to the sky saying: 'In the name of the Moon, of the stars and of the Sun, I bless this oil.'

A personal protection oil can be made by blending the oils of rosemary, rose geranium and cypress together, and adding it to your bathwater. Soaking in specific scents in a specially prepared bath can be an important way of boosting your magical receptivity. A bath of purification is the traditional prelude to spellcasting and it is prepared by adding to a small cloth bag equal parts of vervain, garden mint, basil, thyme, fennel, lavender, rosemary, hyssop and valerian, together with a sprinkling of sea salt to the water. Illuminate your bath with the light of a white candle set in a crystal holder, then lie back, squeeze the herb bag into the water to maximise its potency, and visualise the stresses and strains of everyday life simply dissolving away. Afterwards anoint the soles of your feet, your wrists and forehead with the appropriate magical oil.

The Faery Grove

*Trees have long exerted a deep and powerful magic.
Sacred rites have been conducted from time immemorial in hallowed
groves deep in our forests, empowered by their mighty presence.
This long-term planting project can be your magical gift to future
generations. The five trees chosen possess great magical
potency individually. Planted together in a circle, the ancient
symbol of fertility, reincarnation and eternity, they will
provide a truly energising ritual space.*

Plants for the Faery Grove

Oak (*Quercus*)

Mistletoe (*Viscum album*)

Ash (*Fraxinus excelsior*)

Hawthorn (*Crataegus oxyacantha*)

Elder (*Sambucus canadensis*)

Willow (*Salix alba*)

Camomile (*Anthemis nobilis*)

The entrance to faeryland, it is said, lies between two oaks. Be guided by that advice and plant the most magical of trees in pairs. For the ancient Greeks, the oak was sacred to the great god Zeus, and a particular tree, the oak of Dodona was consulted as an oracle. The Druid priests conducted their rituals in oak groves and the first-century Roman writer Lucan described the special atmosphere of one such sanctuary:

'*No wind ever bore down upon that wood, nor thunderbolt hurled from black clouds; the trees, even when they spread their leaves to no breeze, rustled among themselves.*'

According to folk tradition, 'faery-folks are in old oaks'. In Shropshire, it was believed that the tree bloomed over-night on Midsummer Eve, but that its flowers withered by daybreak. If any were gathered and placed underneath their pillows, sleepers would dream of their future lovers.

Witches wore acorn necklaces to symbolise the fertile powers of nature, but the acorns should only be gathered during the day. Oak leaves must be collected at night and they can be burned to purify the atmosphere prior to a magic ritual.

Oak is the traditional host for mistletoe, another potent plant sacred to the Druids, whose priests always cut it with a golden sickle. It has long been used as a powerful counter-charm. Bunches of mistletoe are hung up to ward off evil spirits and it is still considered a lucky plant.

Magic healing wands are often made from branches of ash, a tree revered for its potency from the earliest times. In Norse mythology, the ash was the World Tree. Its branches spread over Earth and Heaven, and its roots made a ladder between the worlds. Ash leaves placed beneath the pillow are said to induce prophetic dreams.

The hawthorn is traditionally the tree of chastity. A witch's wand was garlanded with its strongly scented blossom, commonly known as may, for the spring Sabbat festival of Beltane. A dense and thorny thicket of hawthorn preserved the virginal princess intact in the original faery story *Sleeping Beauty*, until she was awakened with a kiss by her handsome prince:

'*Scarce had he advanced towards the wood, when the great trees gave way of themselves to let him pass through ... and what littel surprised him was that he saw none of his people could follow him, because the trees closed again, as soon as he had passed through them.*'